my first PICTURE DICTIONARY

By Lucille Ogle and Tina Thoburn
Illustrated by Hilary Knight

AVON

Introduction

My First Picture Dictionary is specially designed for young children who are beginning to explore the meanings, sounds and printed forms of their language. Its purpose is to help them acquire knowledge about 1500 words and the ways these words are used in communicating about people, places, objects and actions.

It is our belief that the most effective means of helping beginners learn about words is to involve them in enjoyable activities that lead them to use the words. Accordingly, we have organized many of the words selected for inclusion in the book into forty-five natural categories and built around them a variety of identification, matching, classification and comparison games.

The broad scope of categories and the delightful artwork of Hilary Knight aim to capture the interest of every child. A trip to the zoo, a visit to the pet shop, a look round an international airport, a glimpse of what goes on underground — these are all scenes that will stretch the imagination. In addition there is plenty to interest the budding naturalist, with categories on animals in general, as well as birds and insects, a look at plants and, more specifically, flowers, and a study of life on mountains, deserts and the sea.

For the early reader there are twenty-six alphabetical categories which illustrate the shapes and sounds of letters and show their proper order. Each alphabet page shows a variety of words that begin with the given letter. The sound or sounds commonly associated with each letter are clearly illustrated. For example, the A page contains words beginning with three different sounds — apple, apron, autograph.

Categories

The words selected for inclusion in this dictionary seemed to fall into natural categories that matched the interests of young children. We felt that readers would derive greater satisfaction and understanding from such groupings of words than from a totally alphabetical arrangement, so we organized the dictionary alphabetically by category, and wherever it made sense to do so, within category. An index was added to help children and adults to locate words quickly.

Activities

One of the most exciting features of the book is the rich variety of learning activities it includes. Children are asked to answer questions, match pictures, compare objects and group them in special ways. The goal has always been to help readers associate words with their meanings. It is hoped that every youngster who opens this book will find something in it that will kindle the desire to learn.

A GOLDEN BOOK®

Western Publishing Company Inc, Racine,
Wisconsin 53404

Published in the UK for Avon Cosmetics by Western Publishing Company, Inc, 25-31 Tavistock Place, London WC1H 9SU. Printed in Italy. ISBN: 0-307-80941-2.

A BCDEFGHIJKLMNOPQRSTUVWXYZ

All these words begin with A.

abacus

accordion

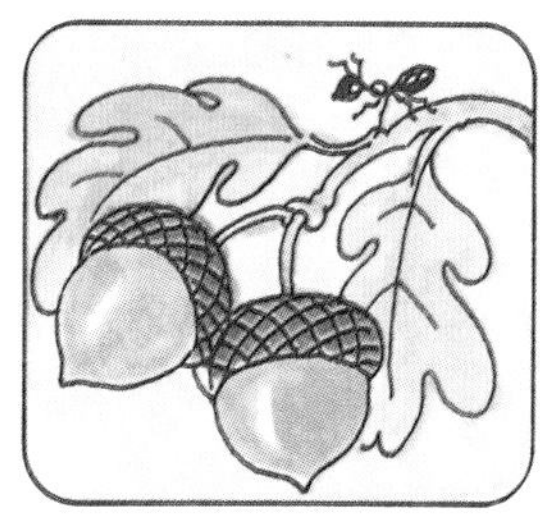
acorn

alligator

alphabet

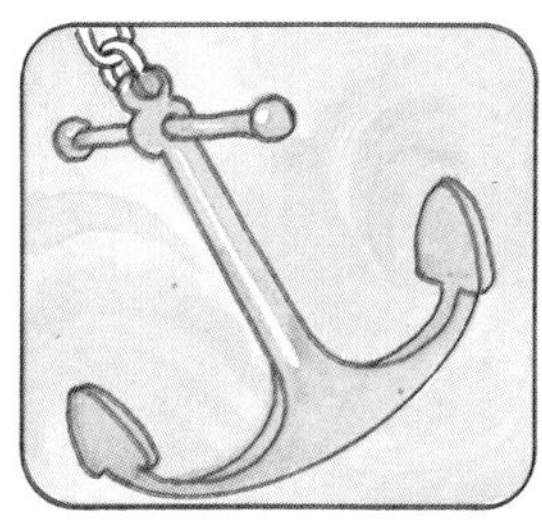
anchor

angelfish

ape

apple

apron

autograph

automobile

Are you able to think of any more a words?

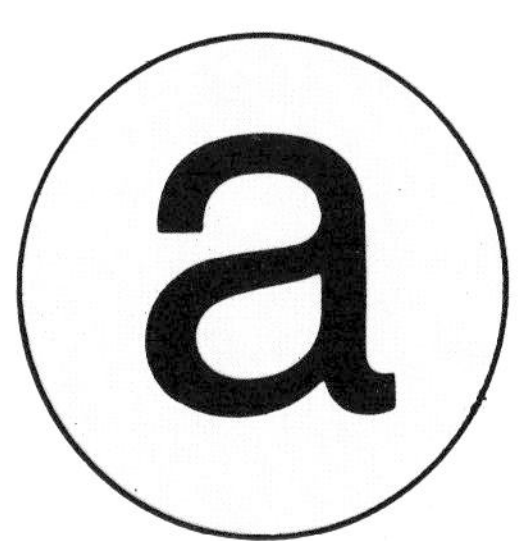

a b c d e f g h i j k l m n o p q r s t u v w x y z

A
a

airport

Have you ever visited the airport?
It is a busy place.
Aircraft and people are coming and going.

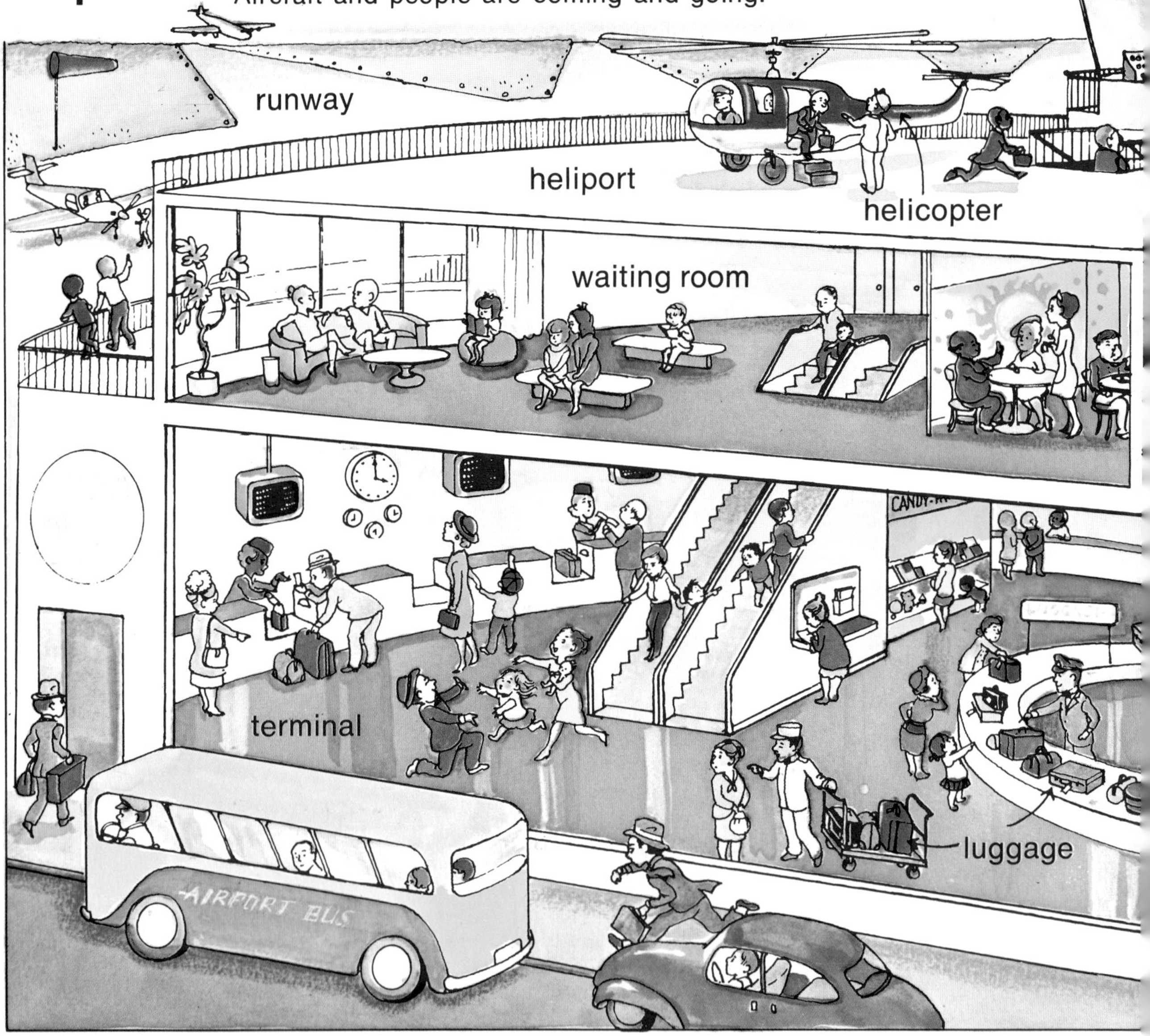

runway
heliport
helicopter
waiting room
CANDY
terminal
AIRPORT BUS
luggage

Find these things in the picture. How are they used?

escalator	suitcases	television	windsock

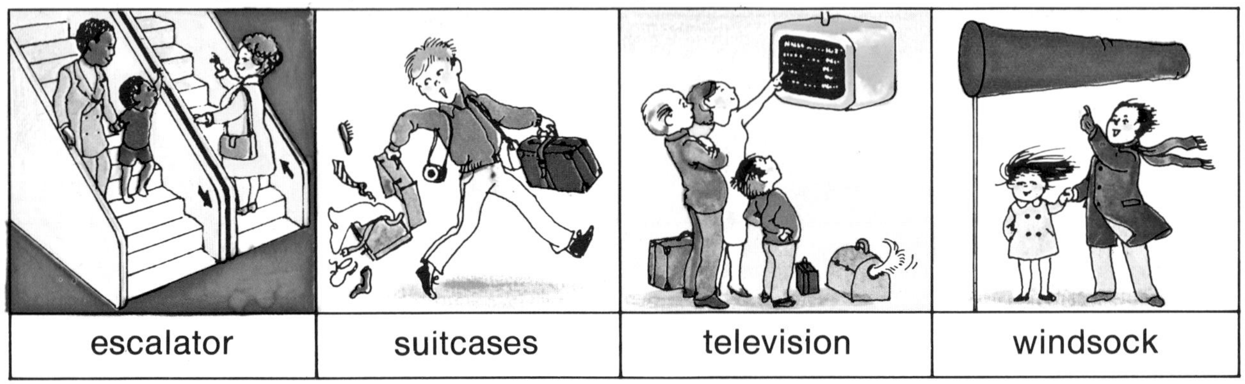

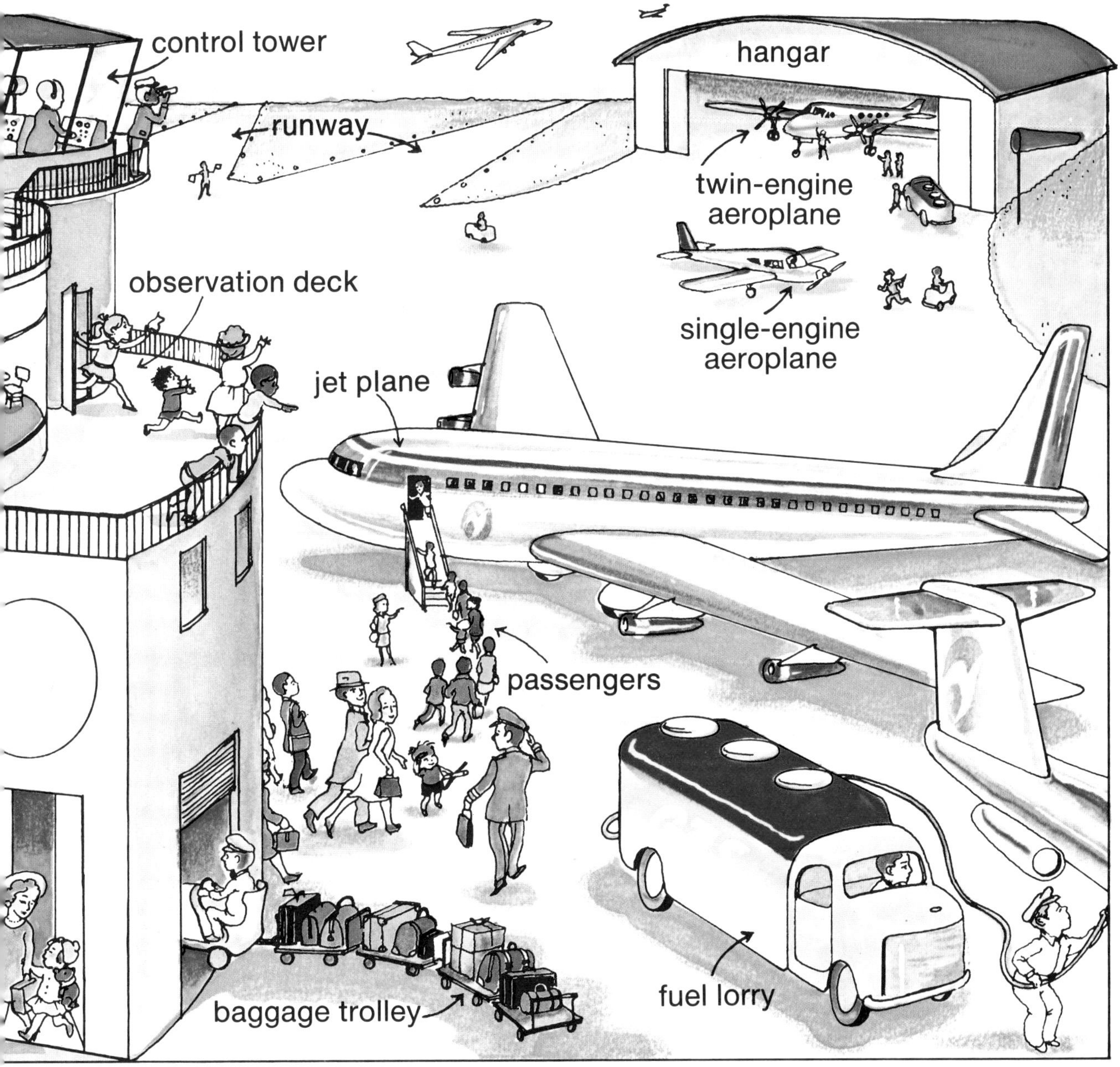

control tower
runway
hangar
twin-engine aeroplane
single-engine aeroplane
observation deck
jet plane
passengers
fuel lorry
baggage trolley

Find these people in the picture. What do they do?

pilot
porter
flight attendant
ticket agent

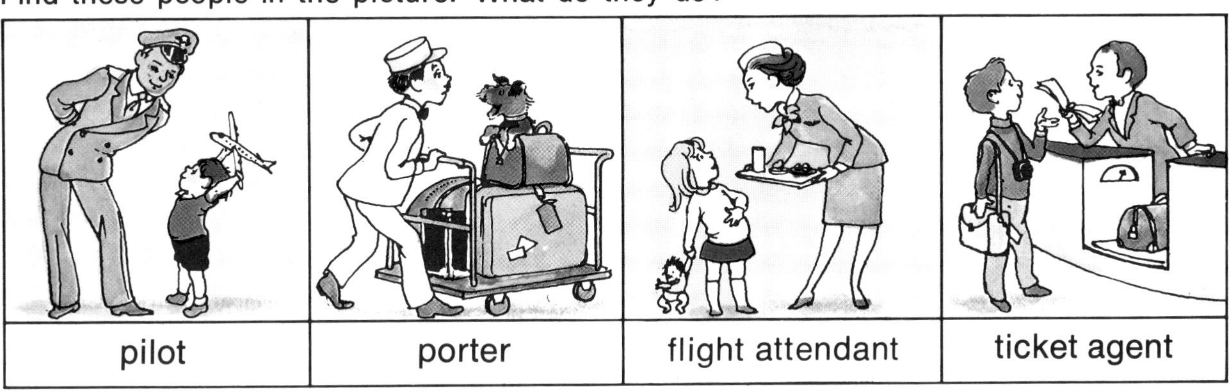

A
a

animals

There are many kinds of animals.
They are different sizes, shapes and colours.

All the animals on this page are called mammals.
Mammal babies drink milk from their mothers.

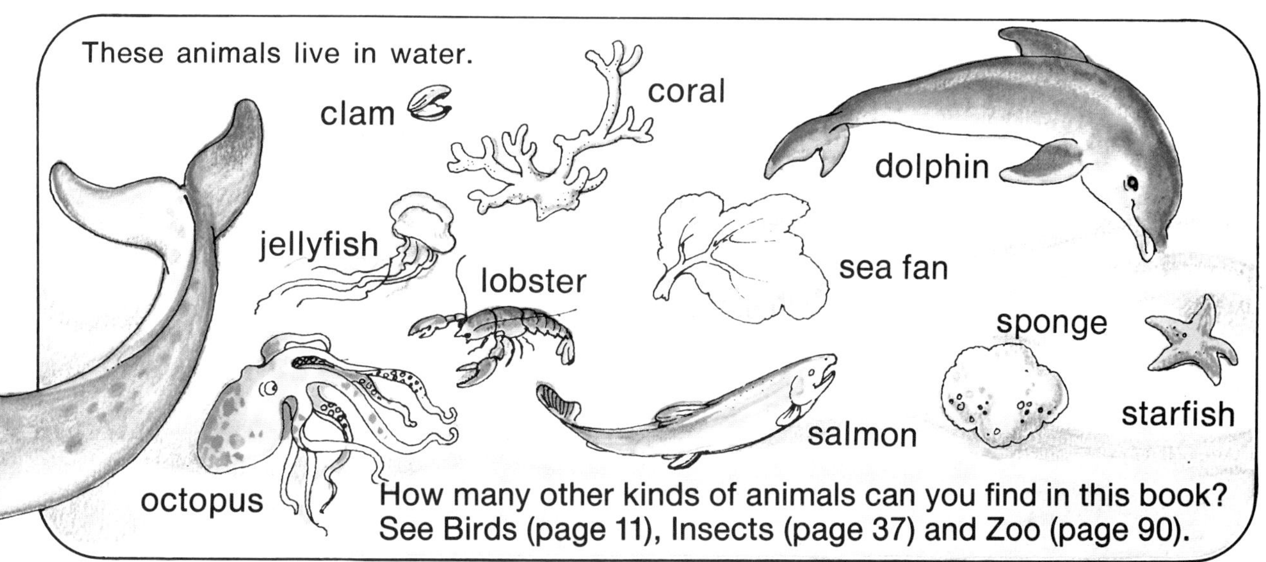

How many other kinds of animals can you find in this book?
See Birds (page 11), Insects (page 37) and Zoo (page 90).

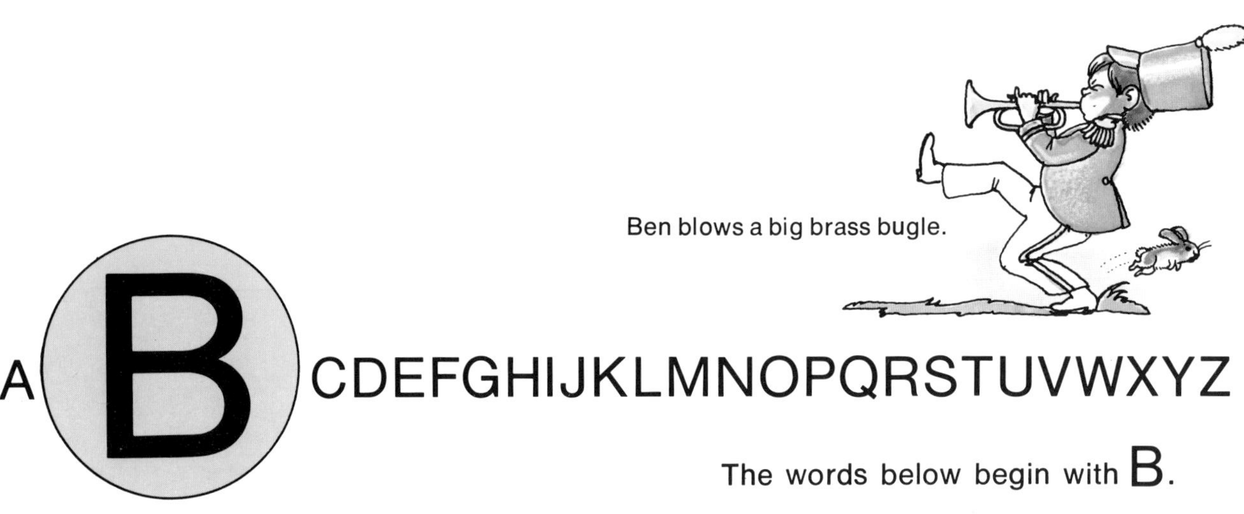

Ben blows a big brass bugle.

A B CDEFGHIJKLMNOPQRSTUVWXYZ

The words below begin with B.

ball

balloon

bank

barrel

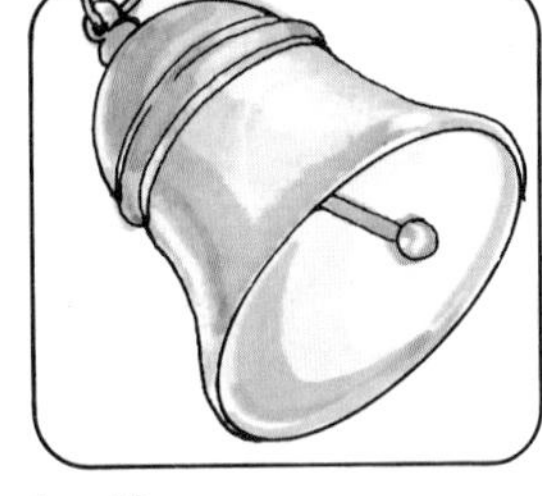

bell

binoculars

books

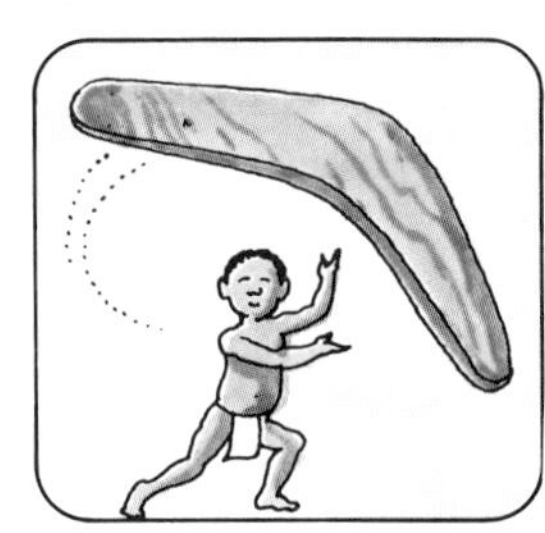

boomerang

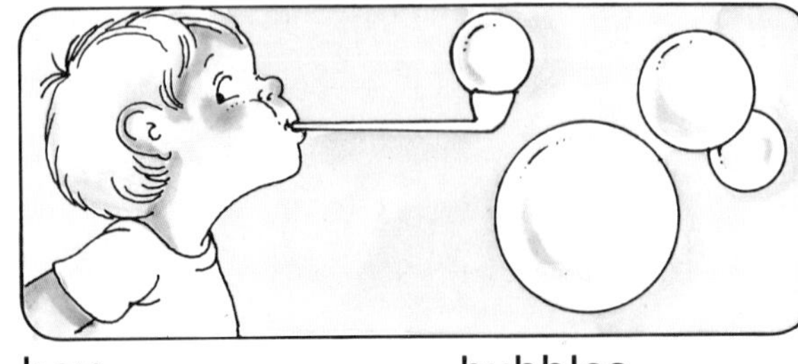

boy

bubbles

butter

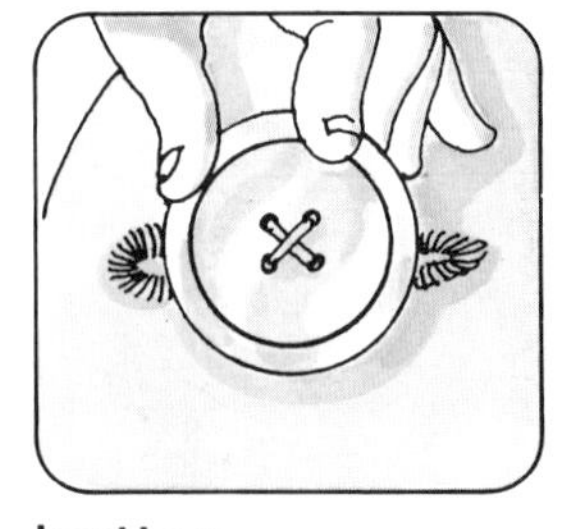

button

Think of some boys' names that begin with b.

a b cdefghijklmnopqrstuvwxyz

birds

Birds have two wings and two legs.
Their bodies are covered with feathers.

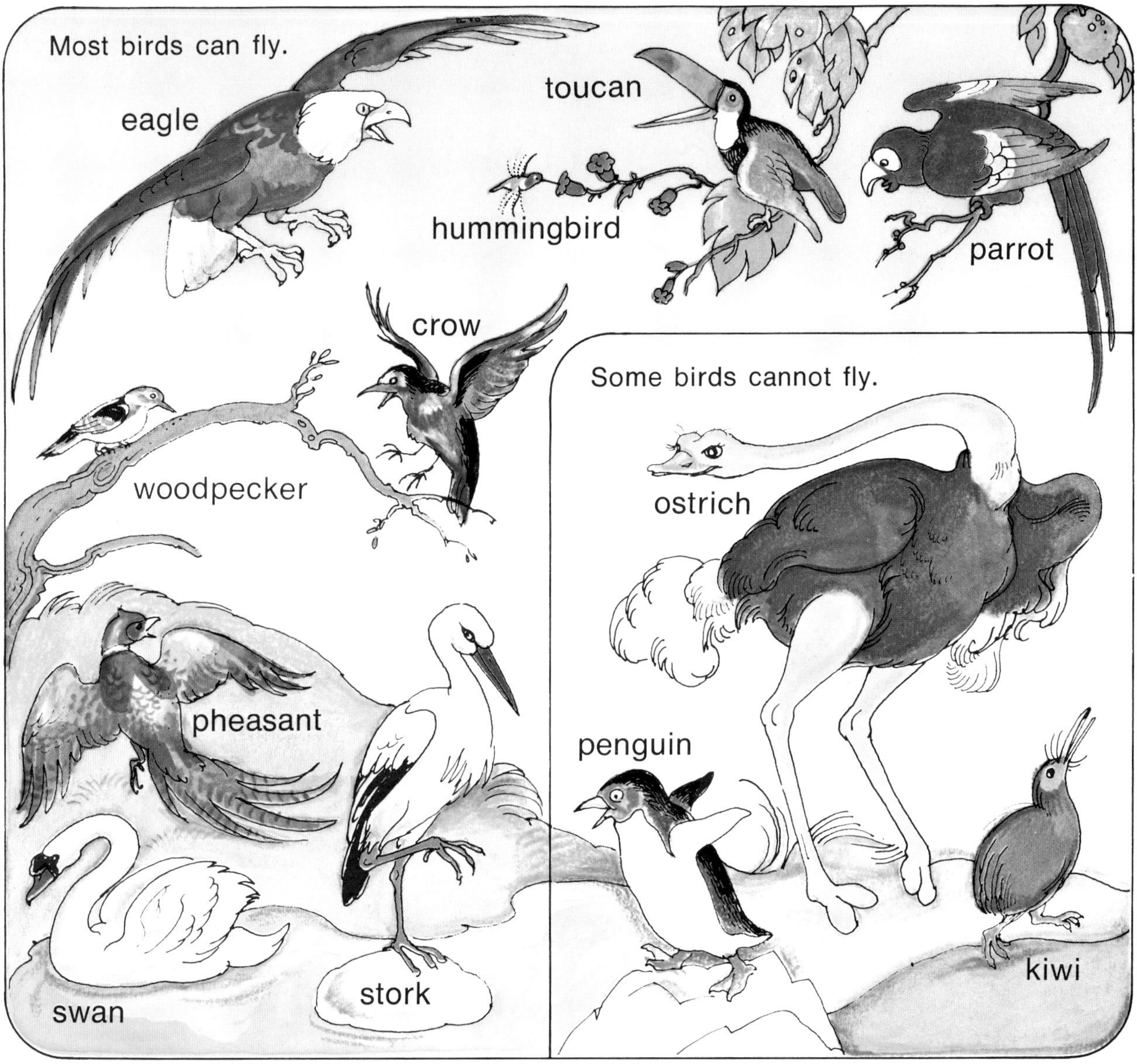

Most birds can fly.

eagle

toucan

hummingbird

parrot

crow

woodpecker

pheasant

swan

stork

Some birds cannot fly.

ostrich

penguin

kiwi

Birds hatch from eggs.

See if you can find some more birds in this book.

B
b

body

My body is covered with skin. Is yours?
My bird's body is covered with feathers.
hair
face
fingers
beak
wing
head
hand
wrist
claws
neck
shoulder
My fish's body is covered with scales.
arm
chest
elbow
back
fin
bottom
stomach
navel
My cat's body is covered with fur.
hip
tail
leg
knee
ankle
foot
paw
toes
heel

How many of these things can you do with your body?
climb
chin-up
swing
fly
slide
push
hang
fall
ride
pull
cartwheel
roll
crawl
swim
bounce
dig
bend
What do you wear on your body? Look on page 16.

B
b

books

Do you enjoy reading books?
Which of these books do you like best?

Carlos carries a canary in a cage.

AB  DEFGHIJKLMNOPQRSTUVWXYZ

Here are some words that begin with C.

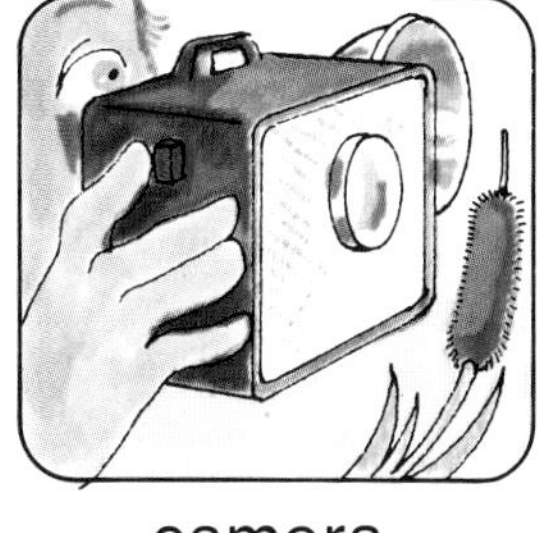

camera

cards

carrier cat

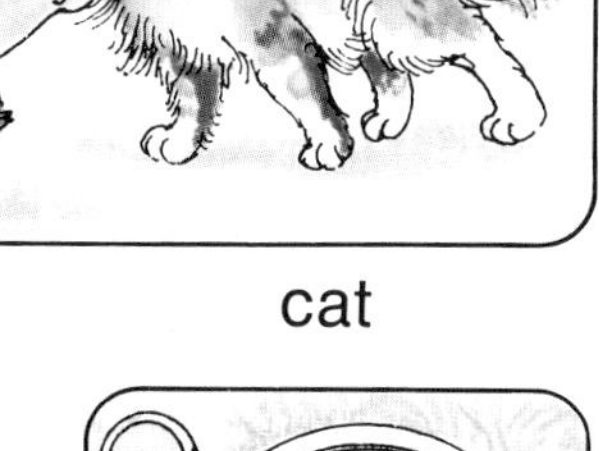

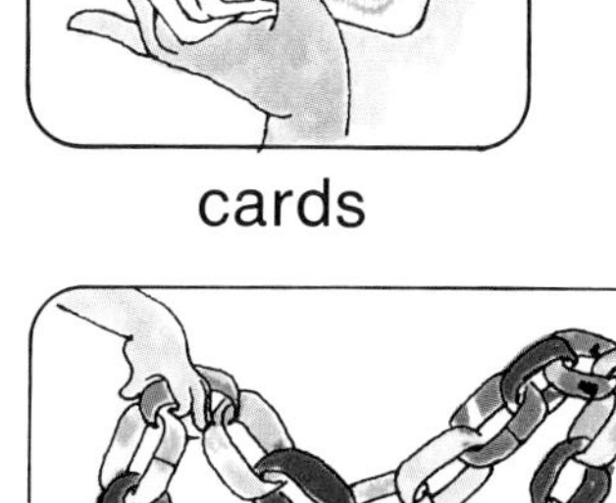

celery

chain children

compass

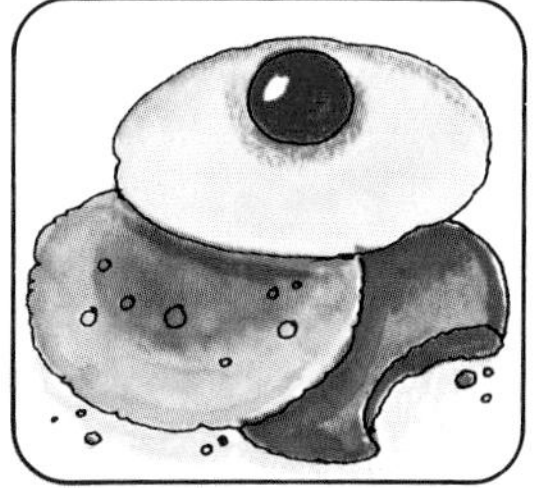

cookies

cradle

cub

cupcake

How many C words can you count?

ab  defghijklmnopqrstuvwxyz

clothes

We wear clothes to protect our bodies.
We also wear clothes to look smart.

Which clothes would you wear in summer?

belt blouse boots cap coat dress

dungarees hat jacket jeans knickers mittens

nightie party dress petticoat pyjamas raincoat rain hat

scarf shirt shoes shorts skirt slippers

snowsuit socks suit sun-dress sweater tie

tights trainers trousers T-shirt underpants vest

Which clothes would you wear in winter?

colours

There are many beautiful colours in the world.

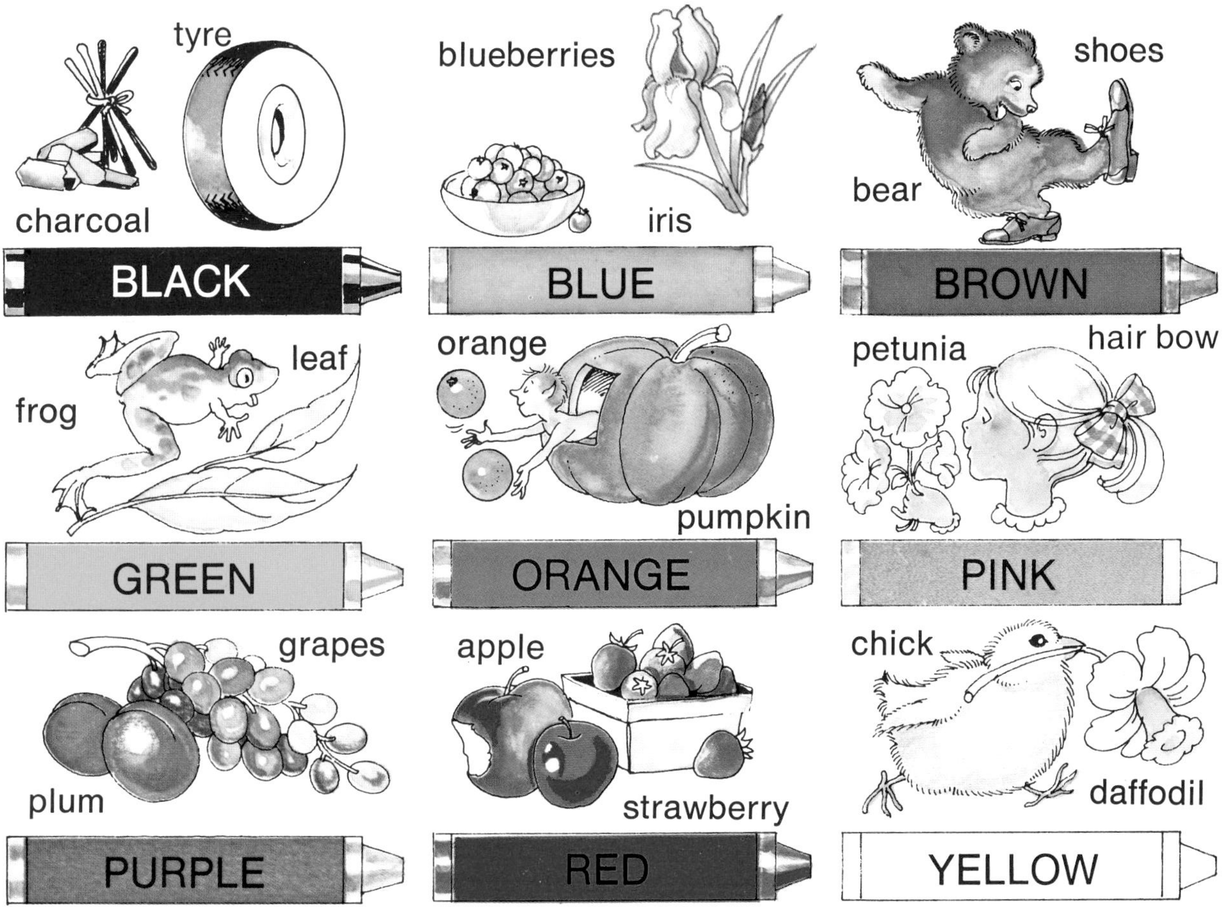

tyre
charcoal
BLACK

blueberries
iris
BLUE

shoes
bear
BROWN

leaf
frog
GREEN

orange
pumpkin
ORANGE

petunia
hair bow
PINK

grapes
plum
PURPLE

apple
strawberry
RED

chick
daffodil
YELLOW

What colours do you see in the picture?

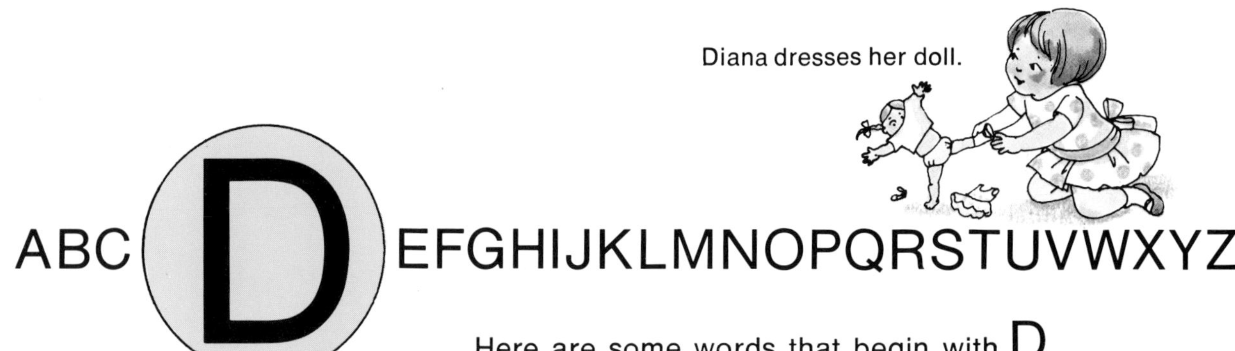

Here are some words that begin with D.

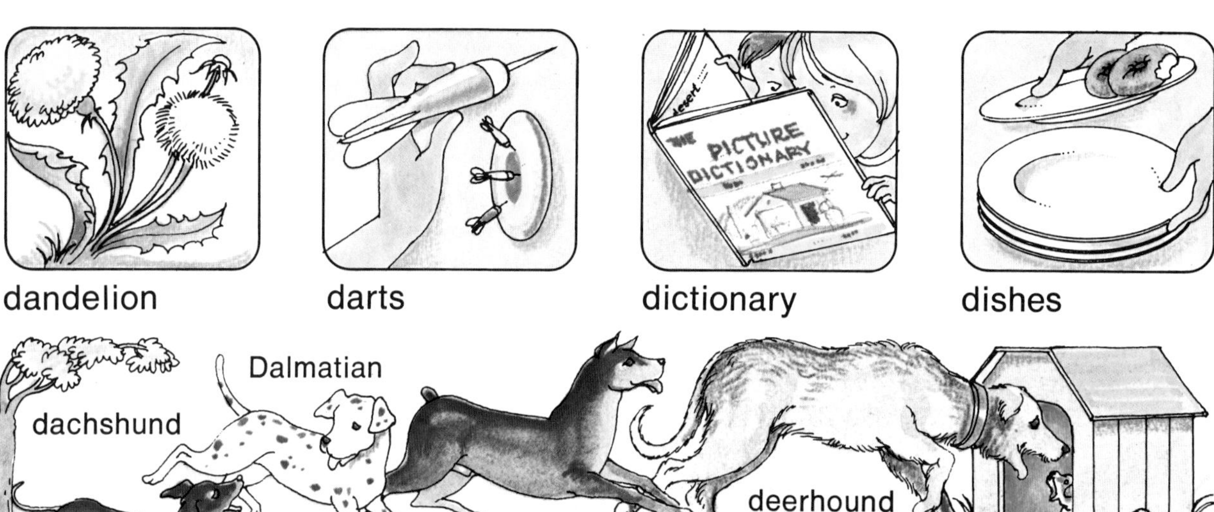

dandelion darts dictionary dishes

dogs

doormat dragon

duck

dumb-bell

Can you think of a dozen different d words?

abc d efghijklmnopqrstuvwxyz

desert

The desert is very dry land.
It is hot during the day and cold at night.

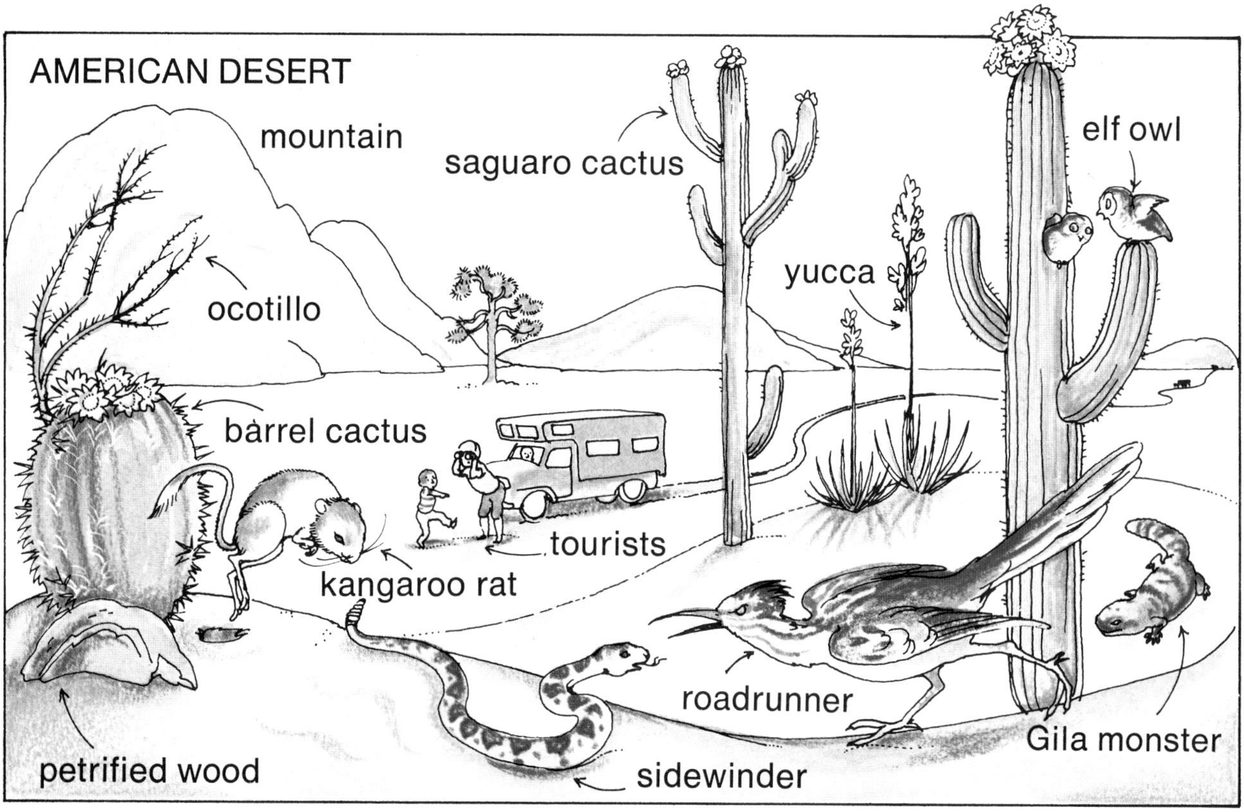

AFRICAN DESERT

date palms
sand dunes
tent
caravan
sheep
camel
oasis
nomads

AMERICAN DESERT

mountain
saguaro cactus
elf owl
yucca
ocotillo
barrel cactus
tourists
kangaroo rat
roadrunner
Gila monster
petrified wood
sidewinder

D
d

dinosaurs

Millions of years ago reptiles called dinosaurs lived on Earth. Most dinosaurs were plant-eaters.

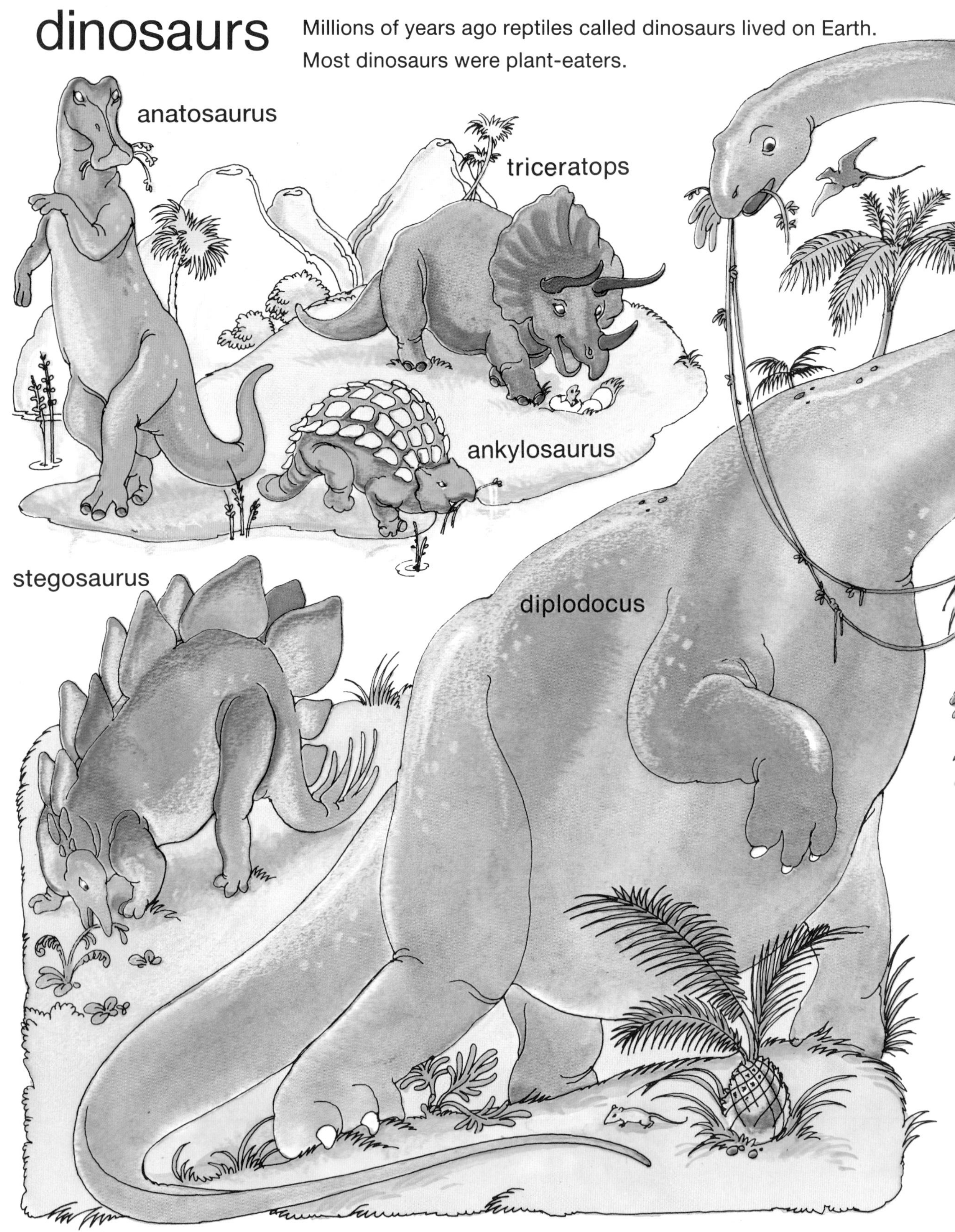

Some dinosaurs were meat-eaters.

No dinosaurs live on Earth today,
but we can see dinosaur fossils in some museums.

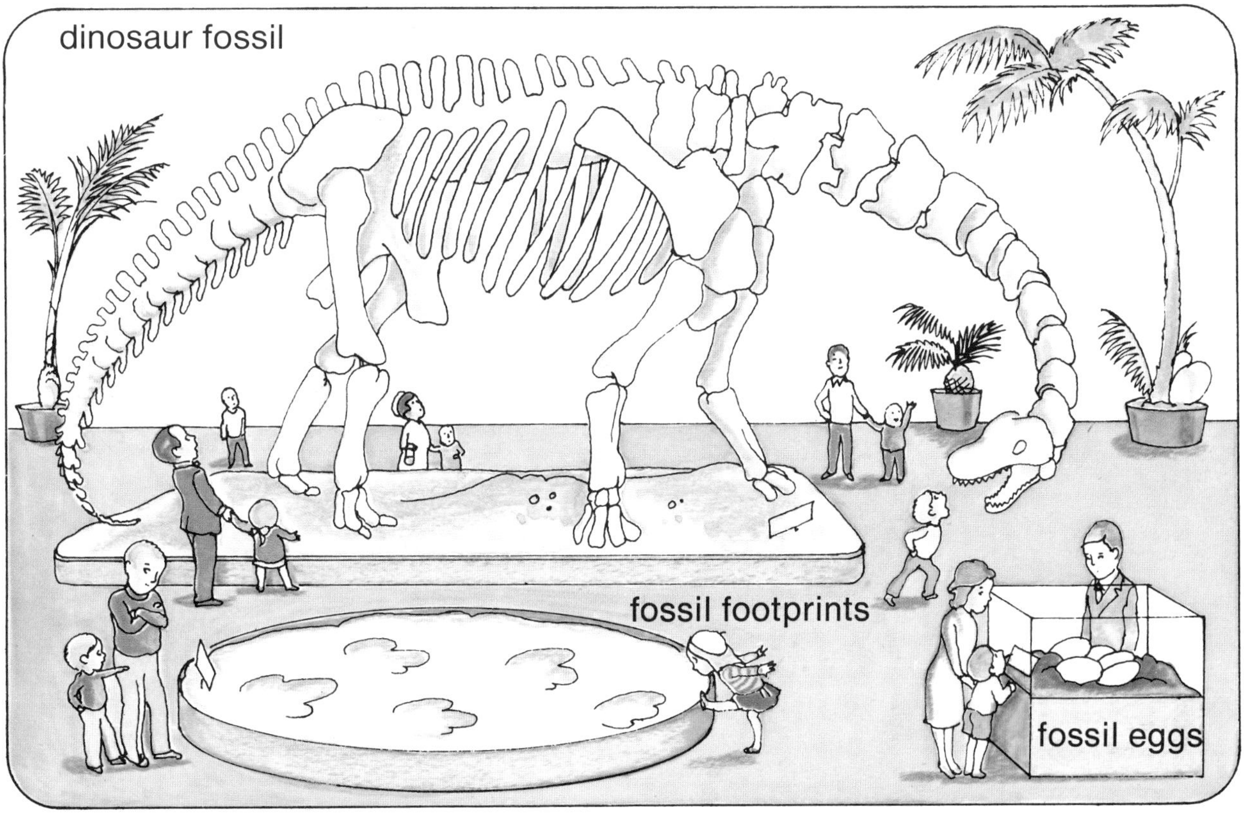

dinosaur fossil

fossil footprints

fossil eggs

Ellen eats an egg.

ABCD E FGHIJKLMNOPQRSTUVWXYZ

These words begin with E.

eagle

eel

eight elephants

eleven Eskimos

elf

ermine

excavator

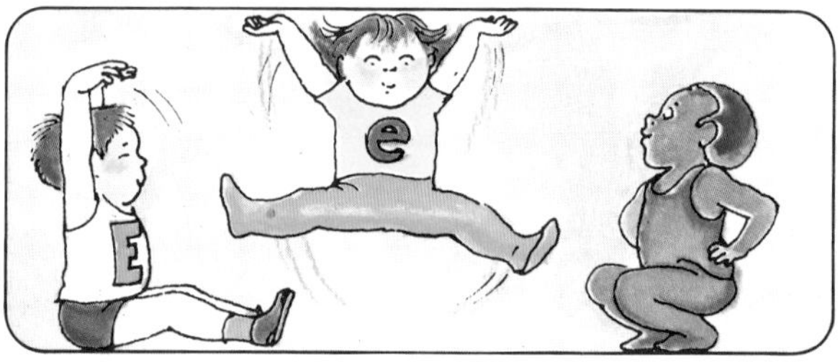

exercise

Did you find some words that end with e?

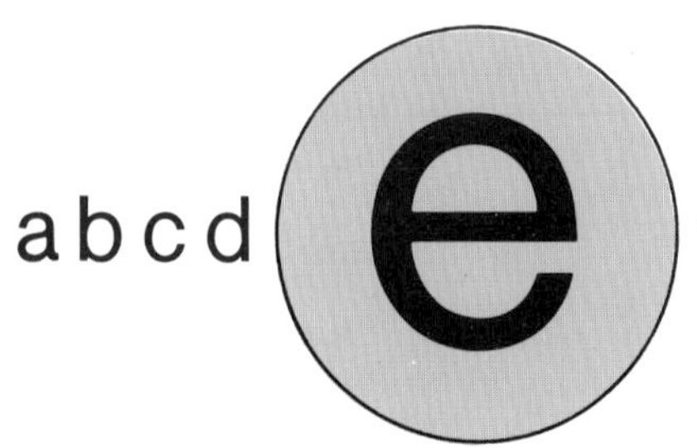

abcd e fghijklmnopqrstuvwxyz

experiments

Scientists experiment to find out about things.

First, make a collection of little things like these.

You can experiment too.

Felix finds a frog.

ABCDE **F** GHIJKLMNOPQRSTUVWXYZ

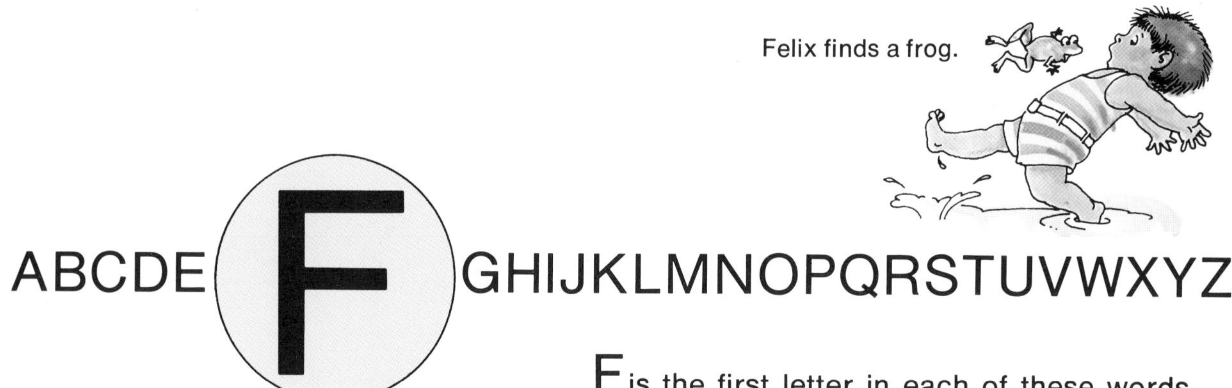

F is the first letter in each of these words.

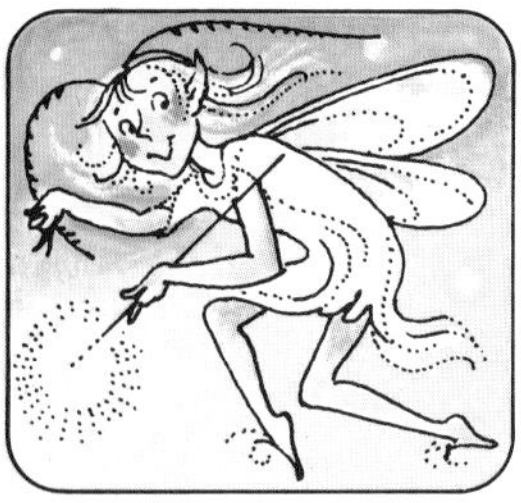

fairy

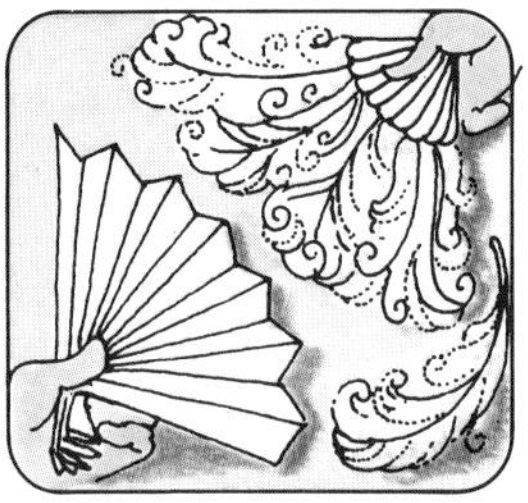

fan feather

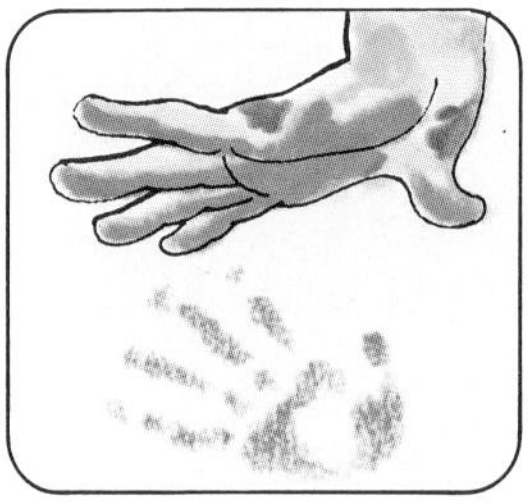

fingerprints

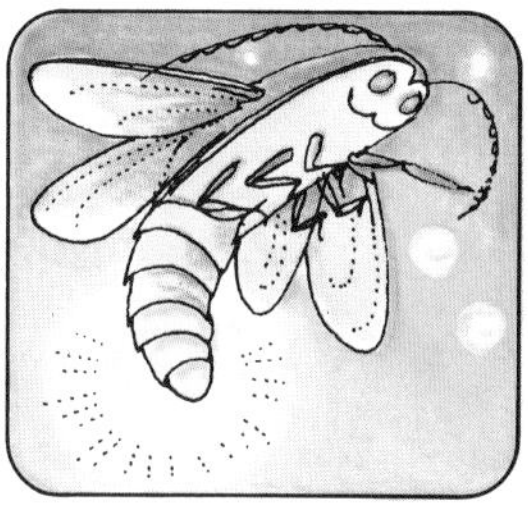

fireflies

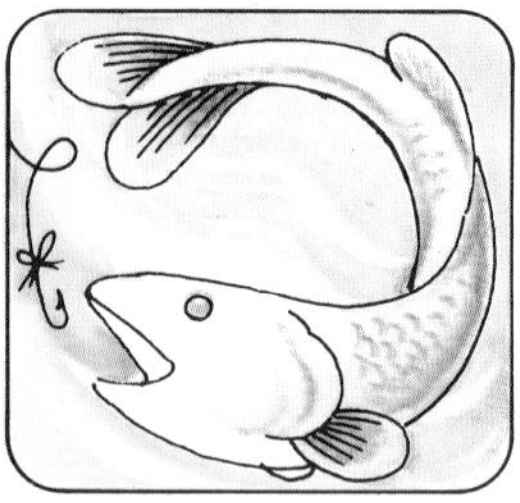

fish

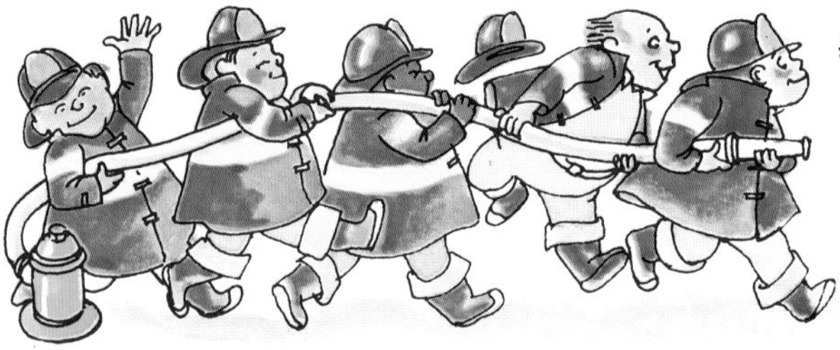

five fire fighters

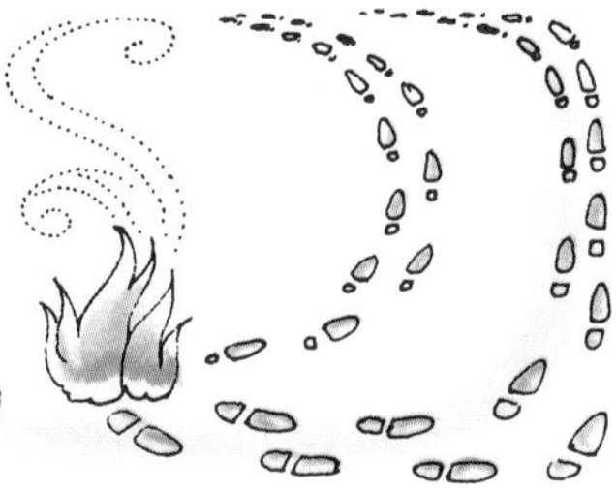

footprints

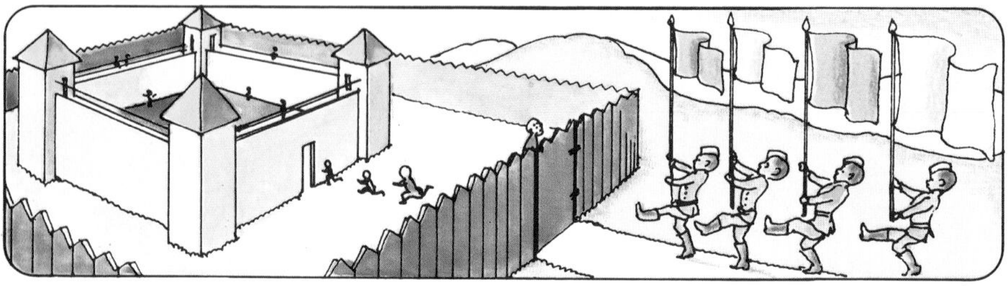

fort fence four flags flying

funnel

Can you find some more **f** words?

abcde **f** ghijklmnopqrstuvwxyz

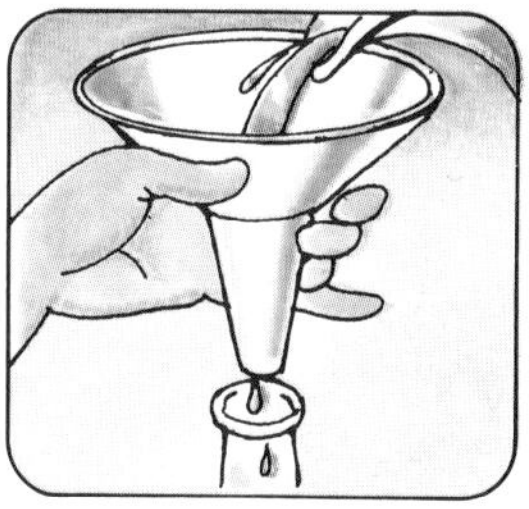

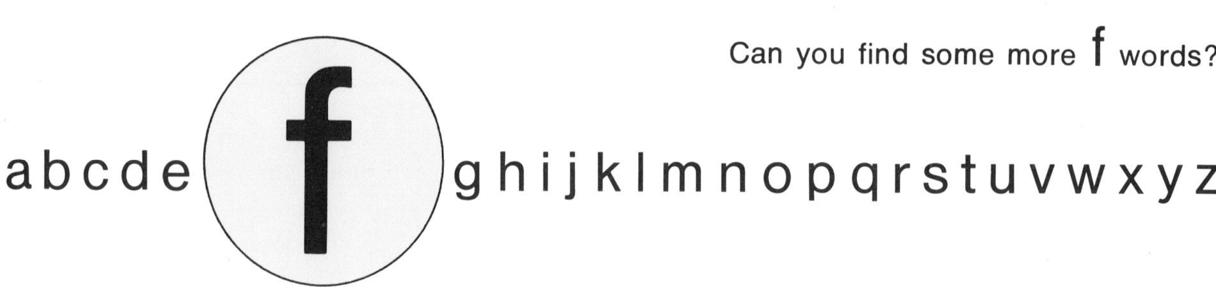

fair

It's fun to go to a fair.

Here are some things you might see there.

F
f

farm

Farmers raise animals and grow crops on farms.

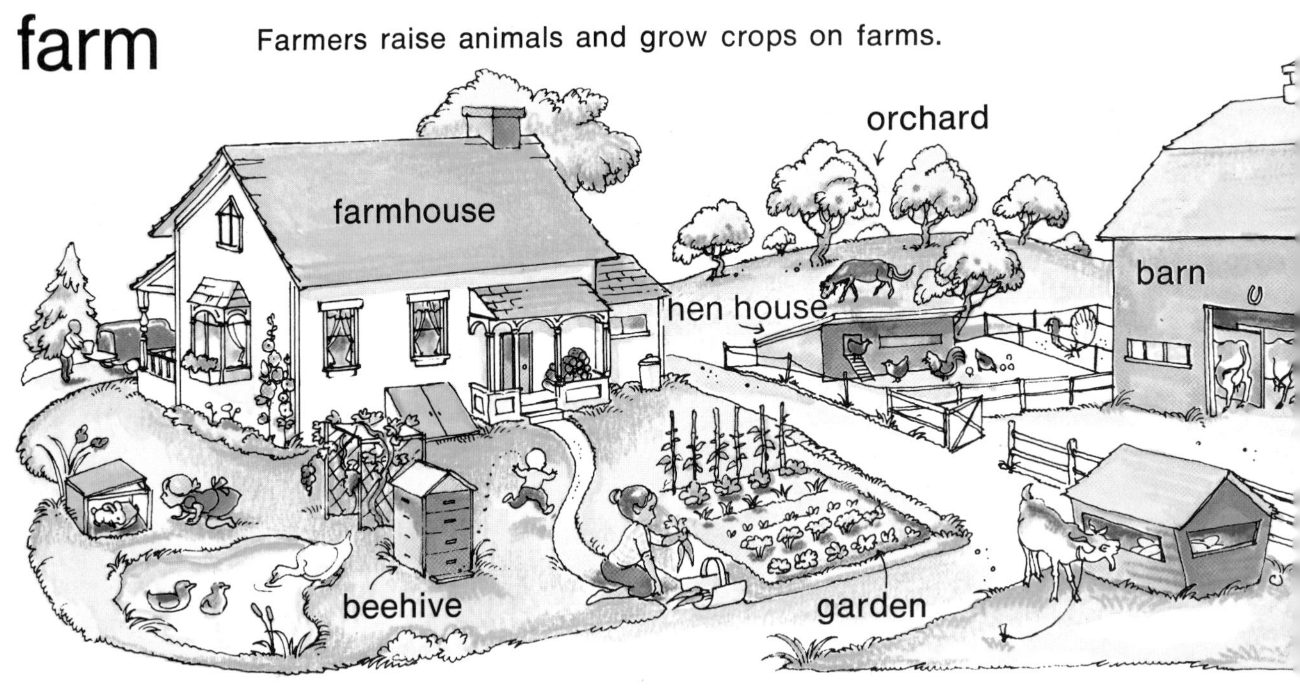

Name these farm animals and show where they live.

Which farm animals give us these?

F
f

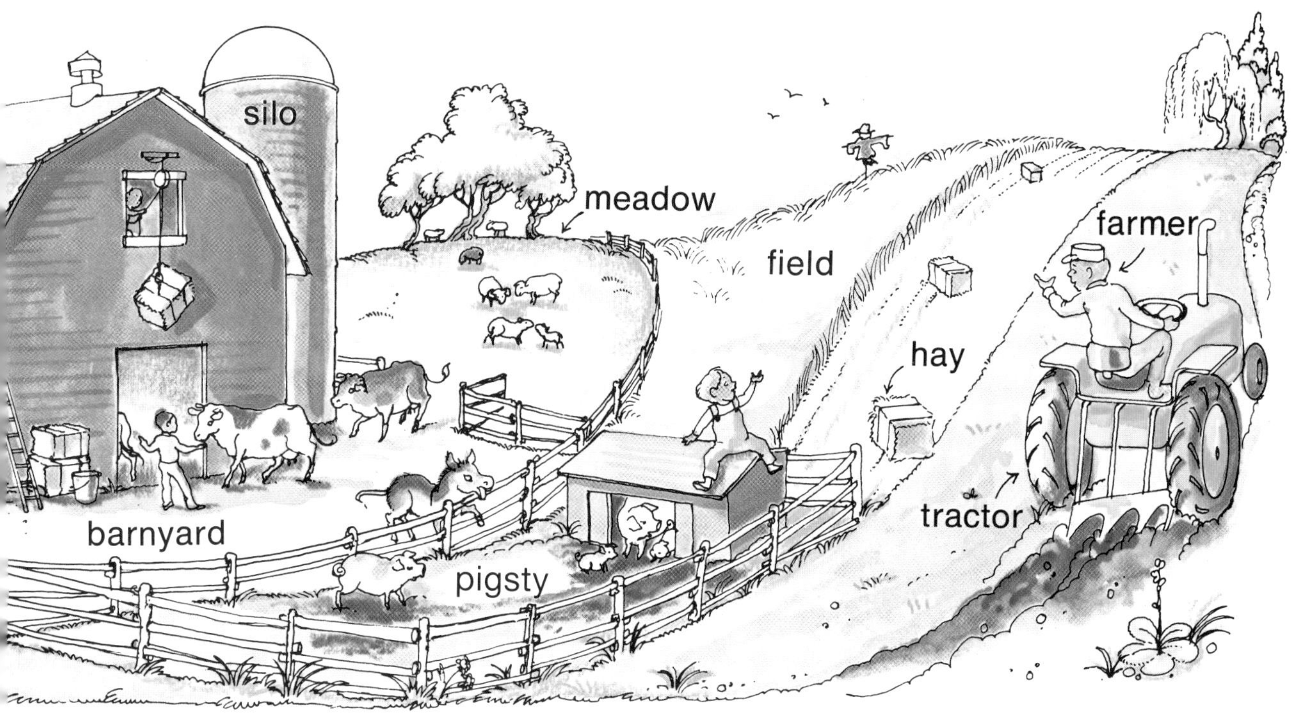

Crops are plants farmers grow on farms.

Which crops are used to make these?

F
f

flowers

Many plants have beautiful flowers.

Which of these flowers are the same colour?

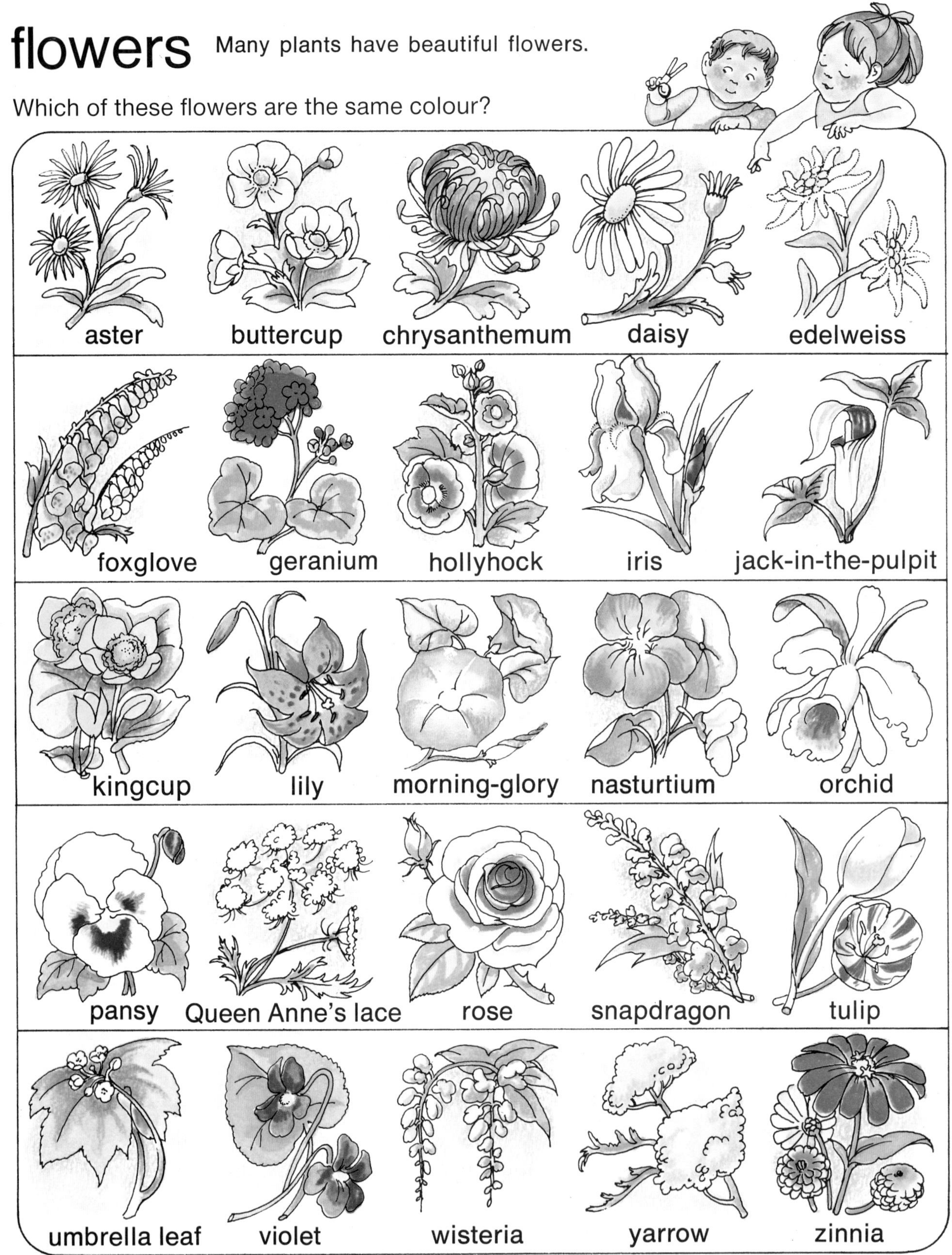

Which flowers would you like to pick for a bouquet?

fruits

Most fruits are sweet and good to eat.
They grow on plants and have seeds in them.

Some fruits grow on bushes.

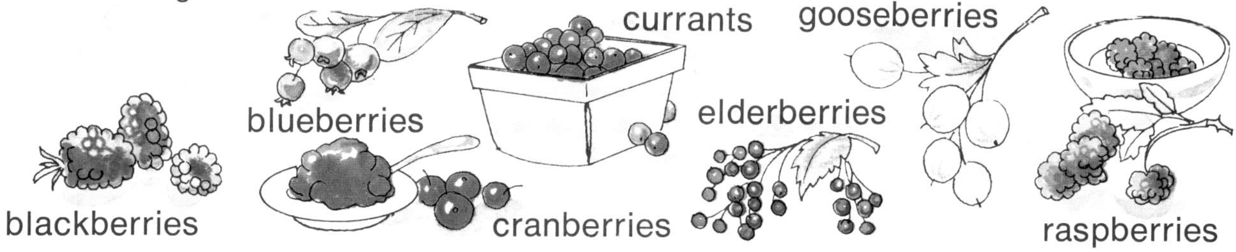

currants gooseberries blueberries elderberries blackberries cranberries raspberries

Some fruits grow on trees or treelike plants.

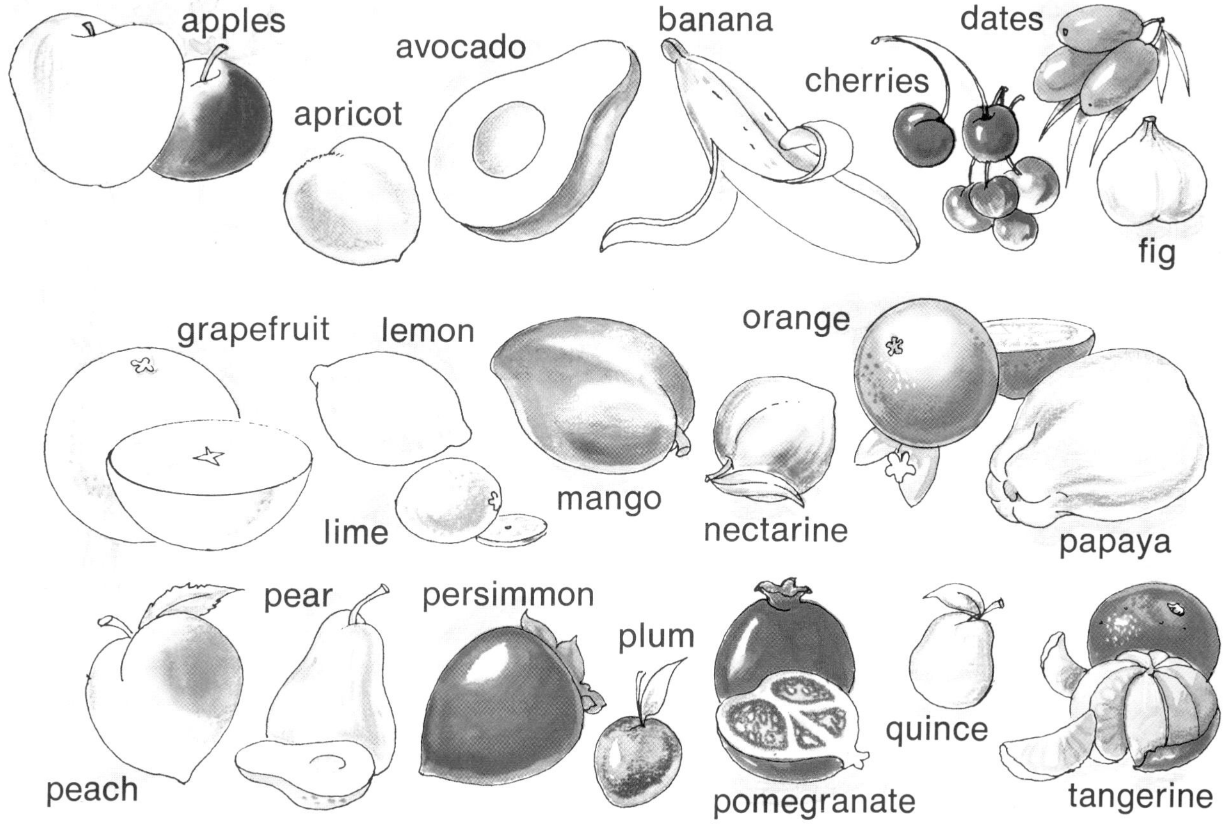

apples avocado banana dates cherries apricot fig

grapefruit lemon orange mango lime nectarine papaya

pear persimmon plum quince peach pomegranate tangerine

Some fruits grow on vines or vinelike plants.

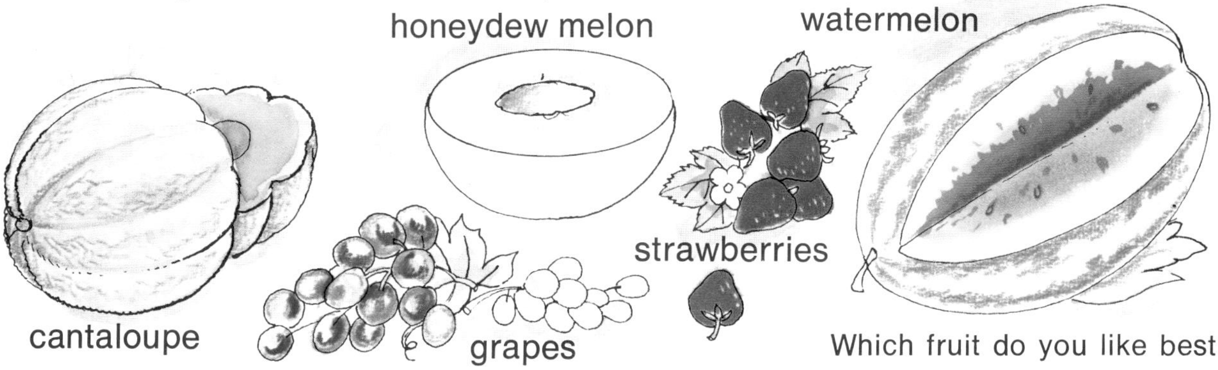

honeydew melon watermelon strawberries cantaloupe grapes

Which fruit do you like best?

Gary gives grain to a goose.

ABCDEF G HIJKLMNOPQRSTUVWXYZ

These words start with g

gate

geyser

giant

giraffe

girl

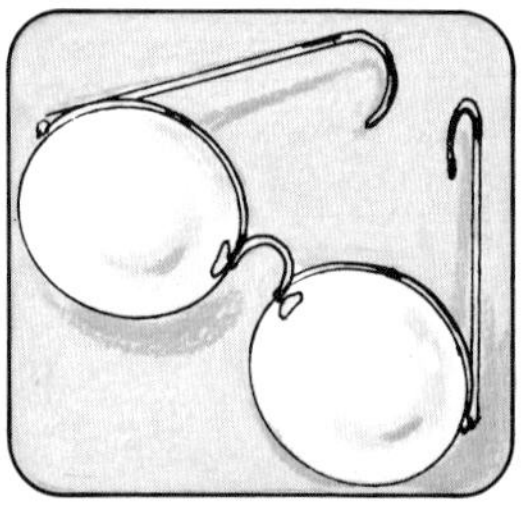

glasses

goat

gourds

green grapes

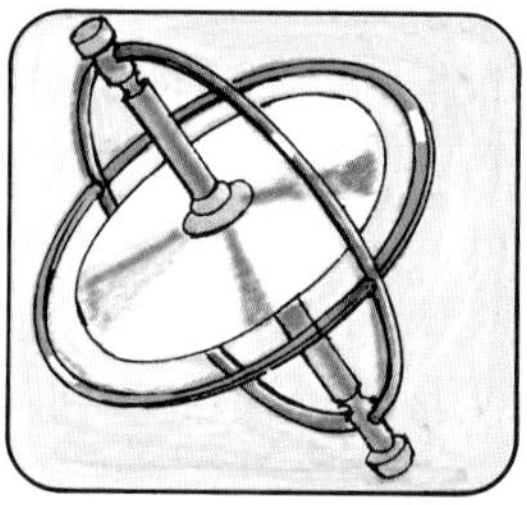

gyroscope

Can you give some girls' names that start with G?

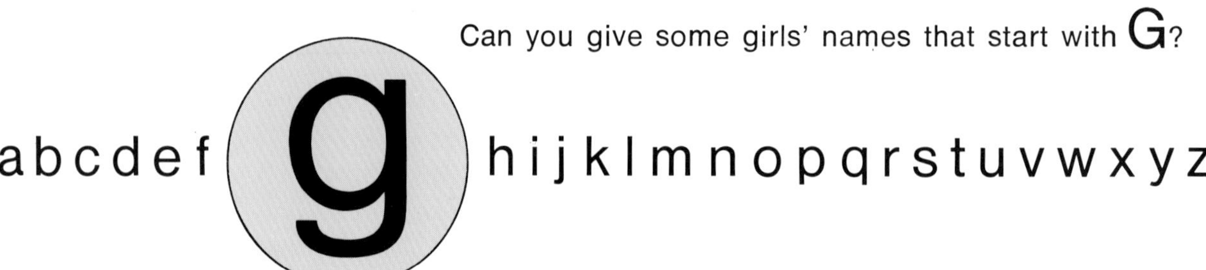

abcdef g hijklmnopqrstuvwxyz

games

Which of these games do you like to play with your friends?

What other games do you like to play?

G
g

garden

These boys and girls are working in the garden.

Henry hugs his horse

ABCDEFG **H** IJKLMNOPQRSTUVWXYZ

Can you hear the H at the beginning of these words?

hamburger

hawk

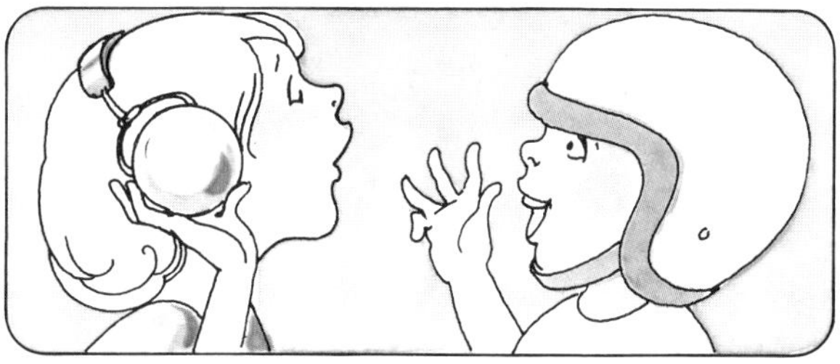

headset

helmet

hinge

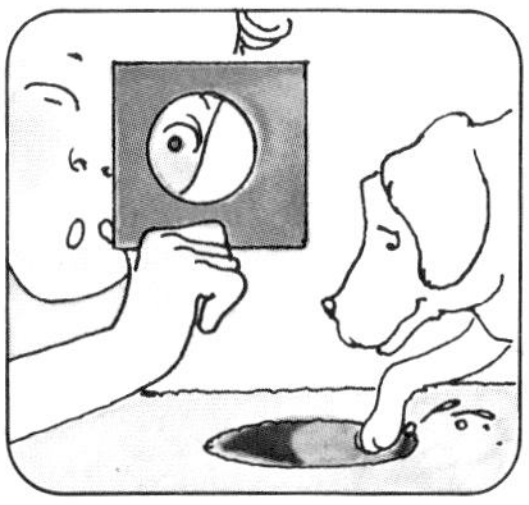

hole

holly

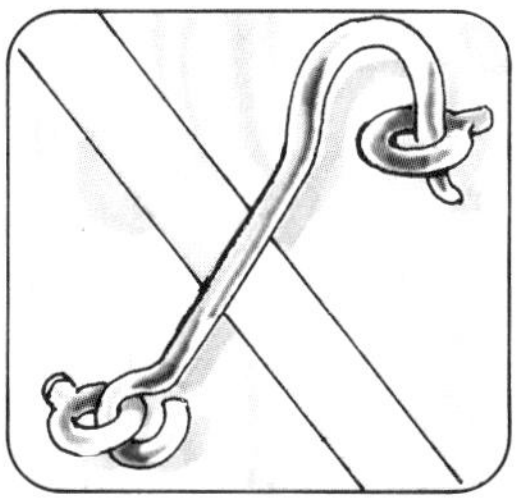

hook

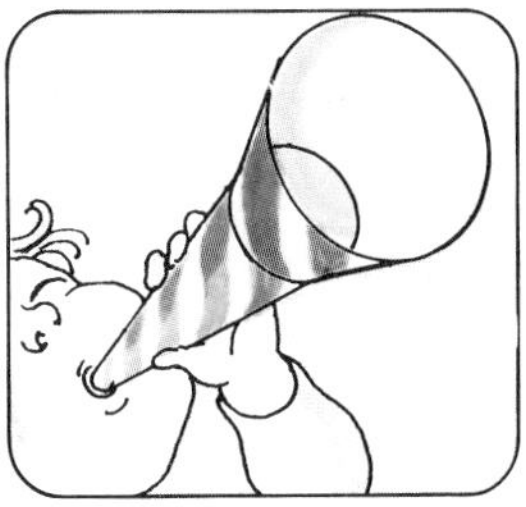

horn

horseshoe

hummingbird

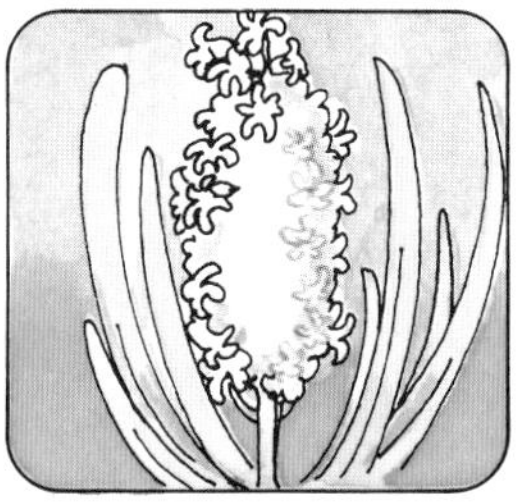

hyacinth

How many more h words can you name?

abcdefg **h** ijklmnopqrstuvwxyz

H
h

homes

A home is where a family lives.

Animal families live in many different kinds of homes.

anthill	aquarium	barn	basket
beaver lodge	beehive	bird box	birds' nest
cave	hollow tree	hornets' nest	pouch
shell	tunnel	web	wormhole

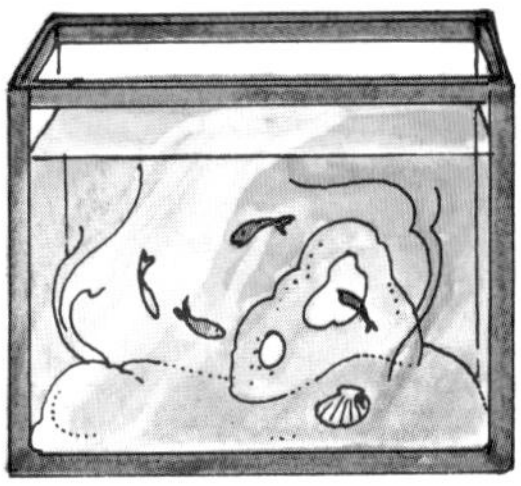

People build homes to protect their families. They often use materials they find nearby.

ABCDEFGH 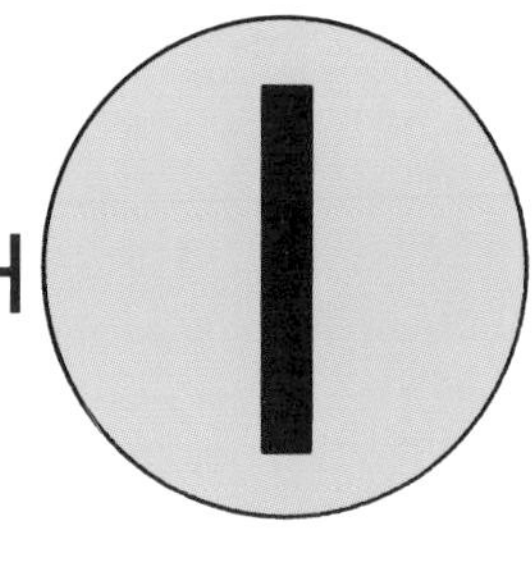 JKLMNOPQRSTUVWXYZ

I is the first letter in these words.

ibex

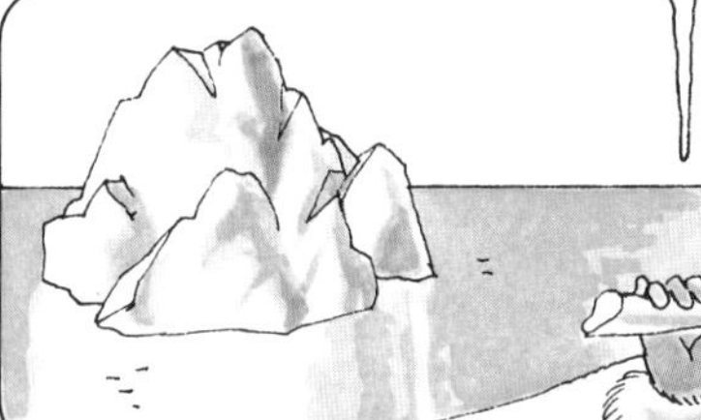

iceberg

icicles

igloo

iguana

impala

incense

incubator

iodine

island

Look for more i words in the Index.

abcdefgh 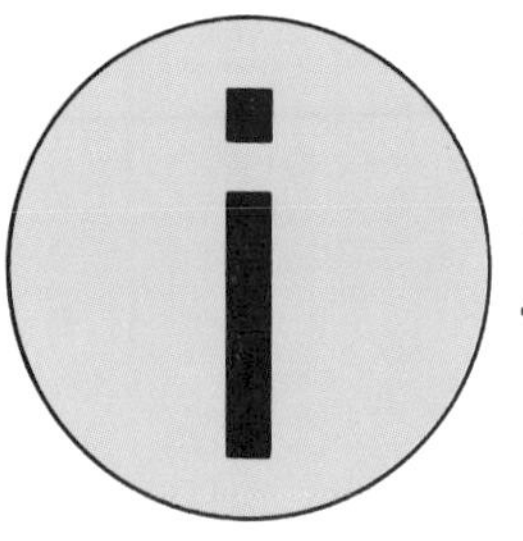 jklmnopqrstuvwxyz

insects

Insects are animals with six legs.
Most of them have wings.

ants
beetle
butterfly
cicada
cricket
fly
dragonfly
grasshopper
honeybee
ladybird
katydid
mosquito
praying mantis
moth
stick insect
water bug

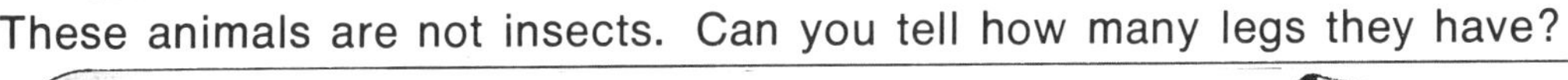
These animals are not insects. Can you tell how many legs they have?

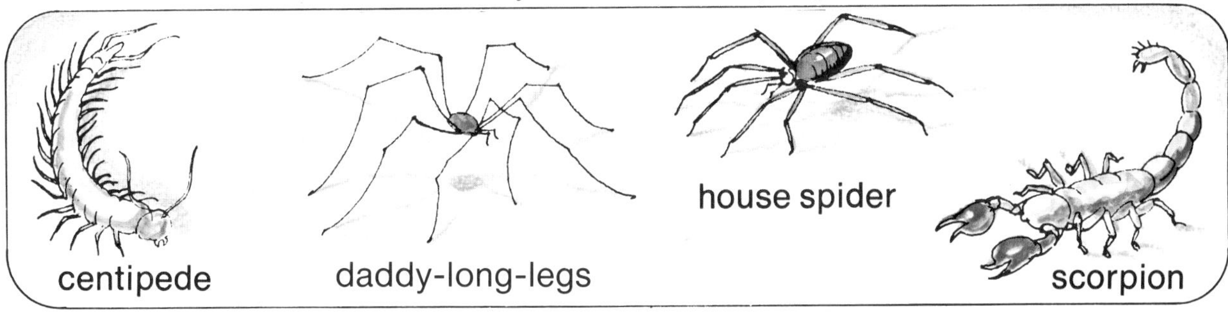

Jeffrey jumps for joy.

ABCDEFGHI J KLMNOPQRSTUVWXYZ

Here are some words that start with J.

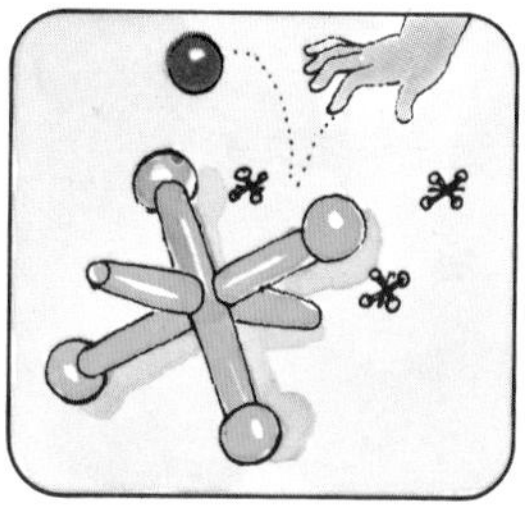

jack

jail

janitor

jars

jeep

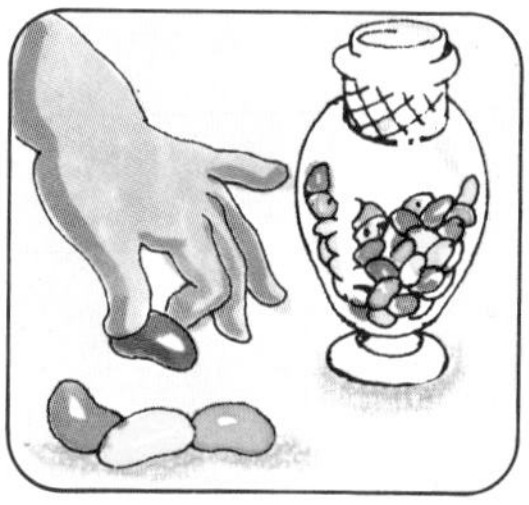

jellybeans

jester

jockey

jonquil

jug

jumping jack

Can you think of just two more j words?

abcdefghi

klmnopqrstuvwxyz

jungle

A jungle is a hot, wet forest. Trees grow tall to reach the sunlight.

Find these animals and plants in the picture.

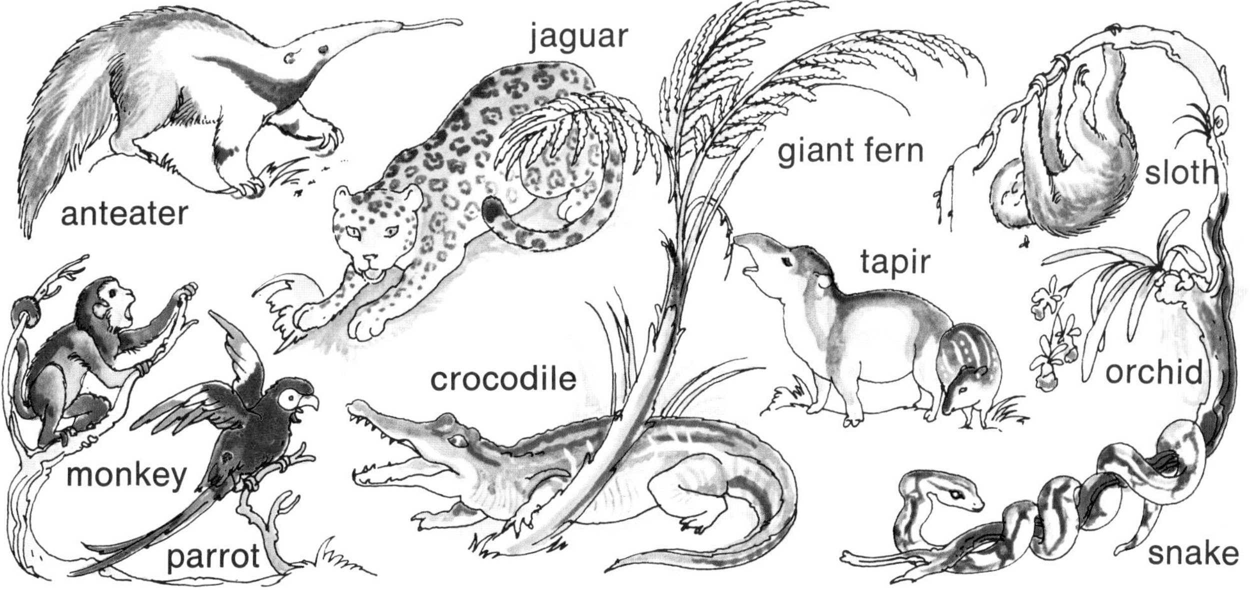

Karen kisses a kitten.

ABCDEFGHIJ  LMNOPQRSTUVWXYZ

These words begin with K.

kangaroo

kayak

kennel

kettle

key

kimono

king

kite

knight

knitting

knot

kookaburra

How many k animals do you think a king might keep?

a b c d e f g h i j  l m n o p q r s t u v w x y z

Laura licks a lollipop.

ABCDEFGHIJK **L** MNOPQRSTUVWXYZ

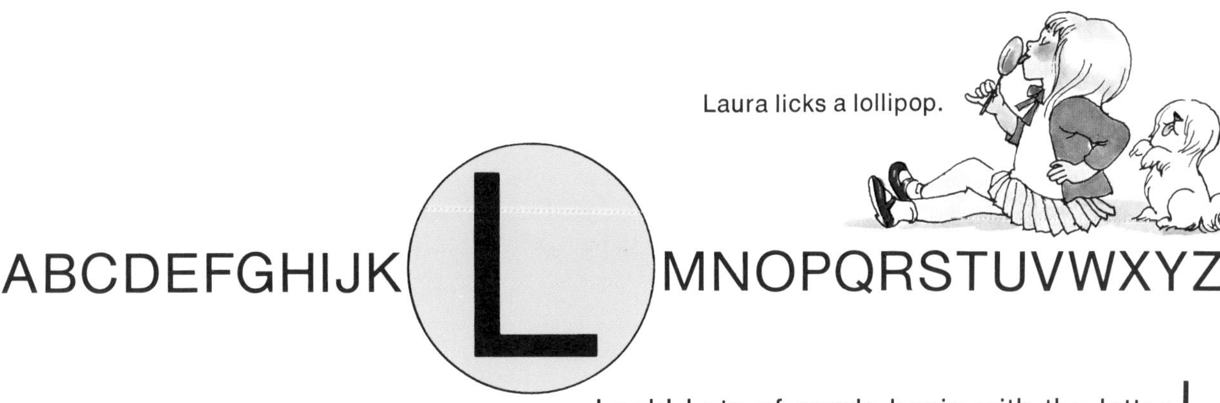

Look! Lots of words begin with the letter L.

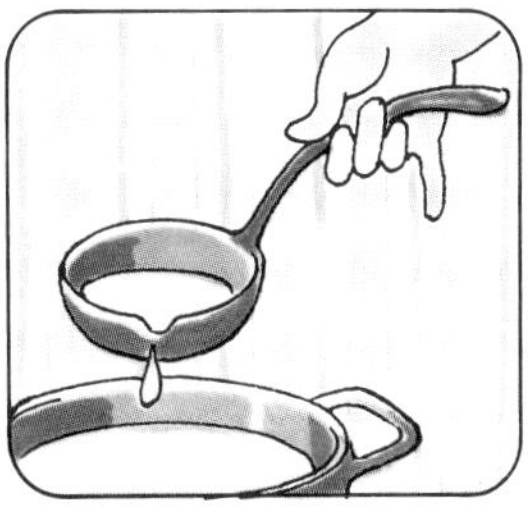

ladle

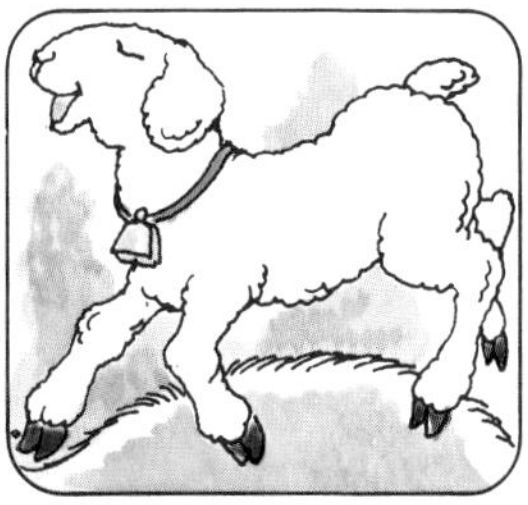

lamb

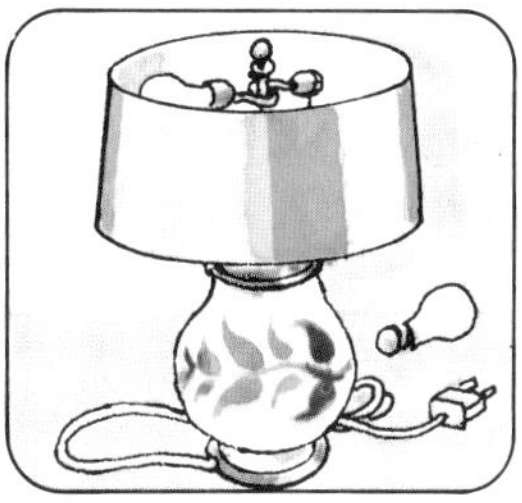

lamp

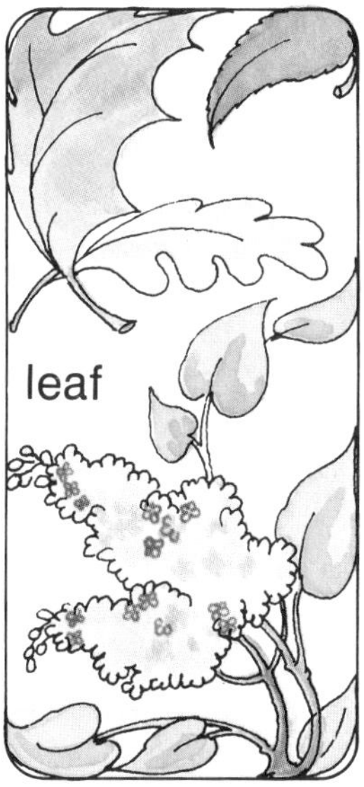

leaf

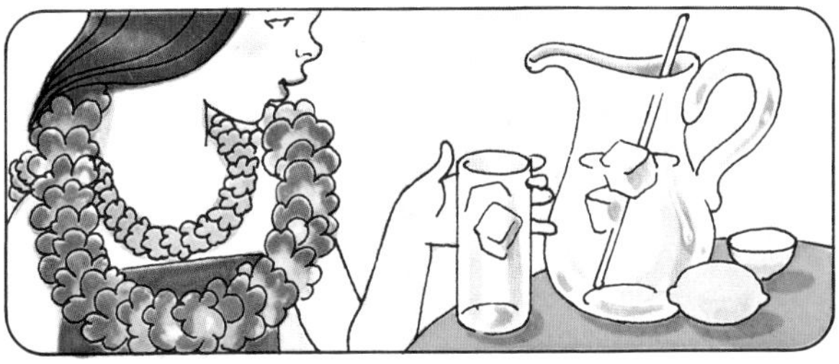

lei

lemonade

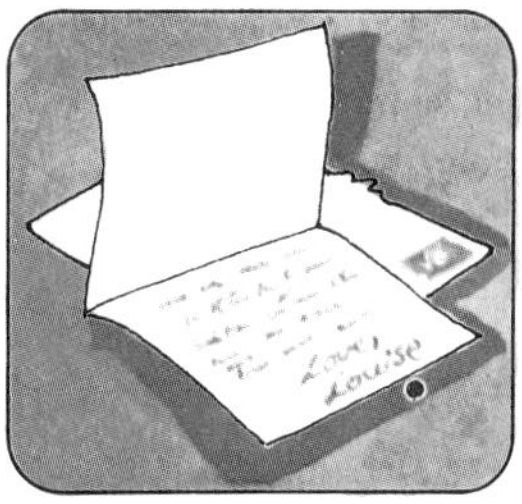

letter

lilac

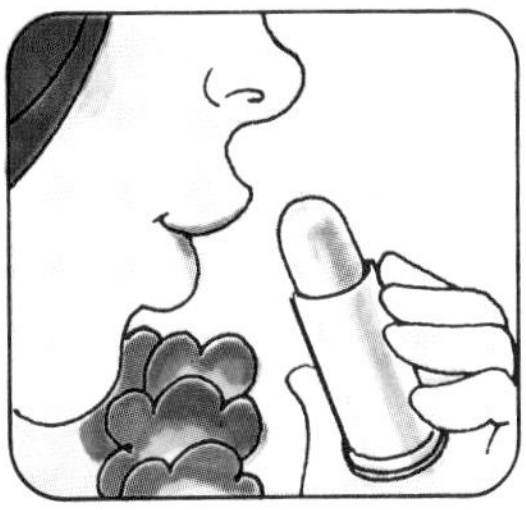

lipstick

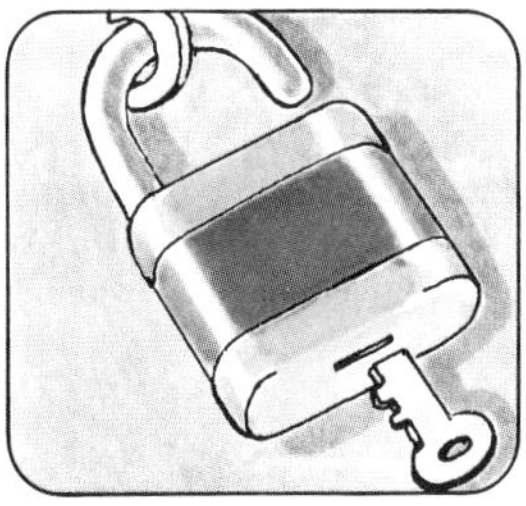

lock

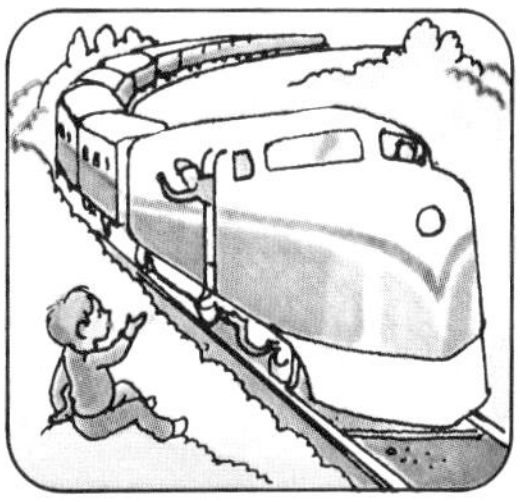

locomotive

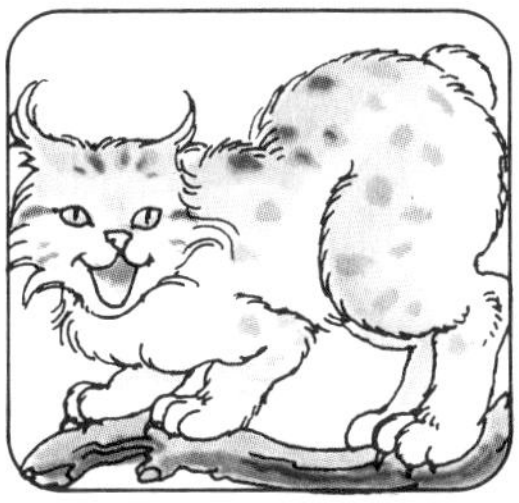

lynx

Which l words do you like to listen to?

abcdefghijk **l** mnopqrstuvwxyz

Let's pretend.

Sometimes it is fun to dress up and pretend to be other people.

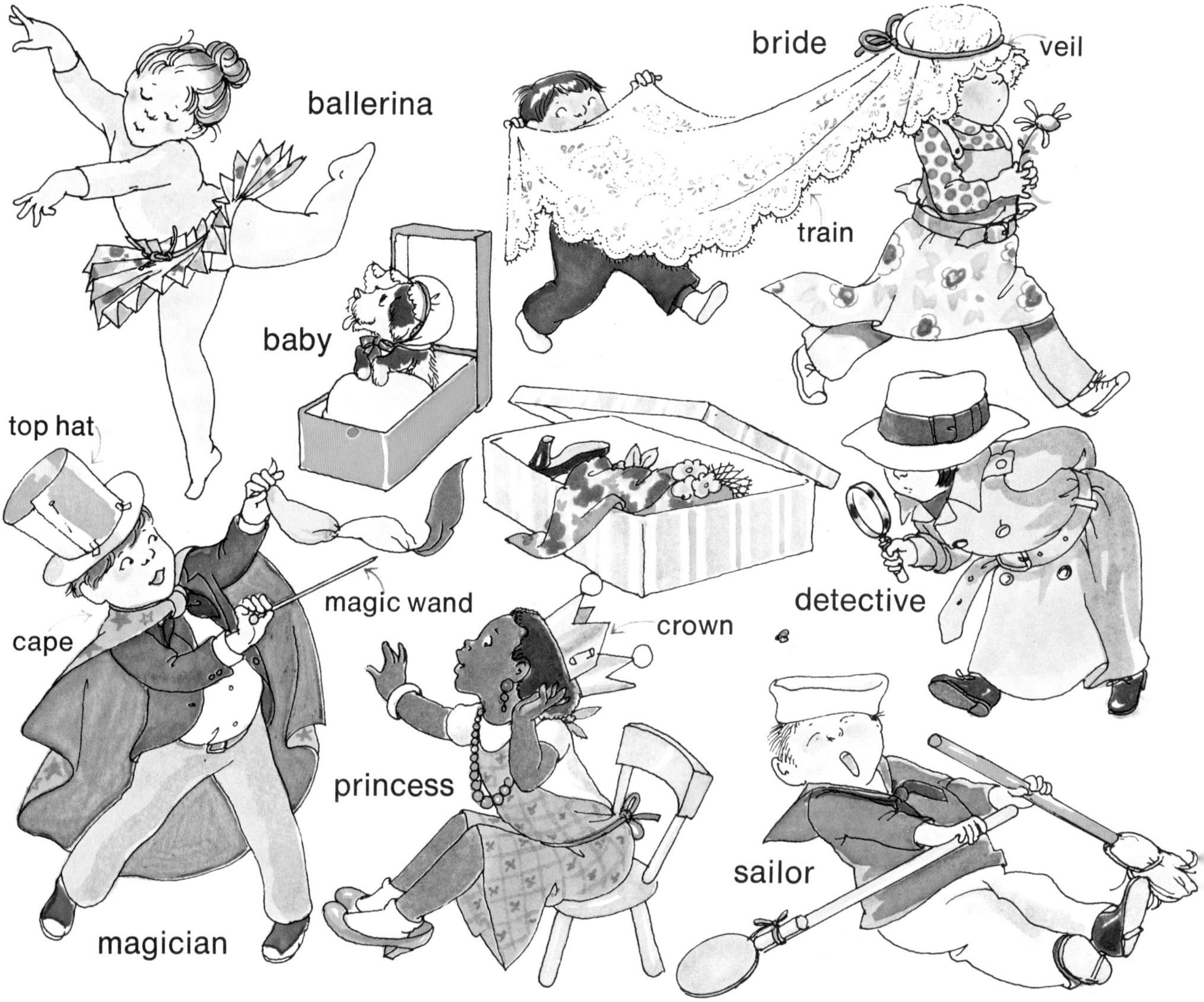

ballerina
bride
veil
train
baby
top hat
magic wand
crown
detective
cape
princess
sailor
magician

Sometimes it is fun to pretend to be animals.

elephant
duck
rabbit
snake

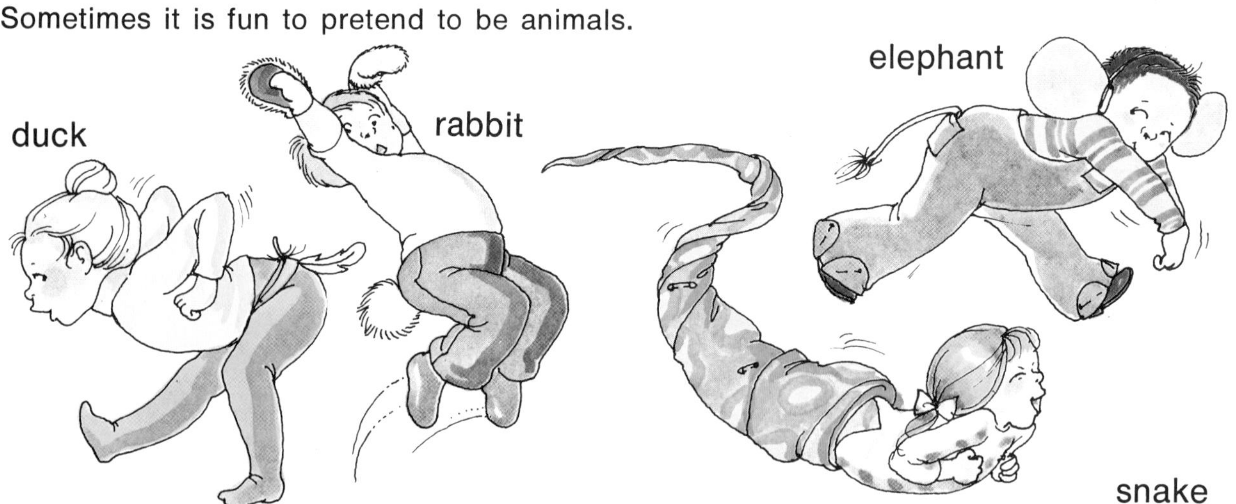

Mike makes music on his mandolin.

ABCDEFGHIJKL **M** NOPQRSTUVWXYZ

M is in the middle of the alphabet.

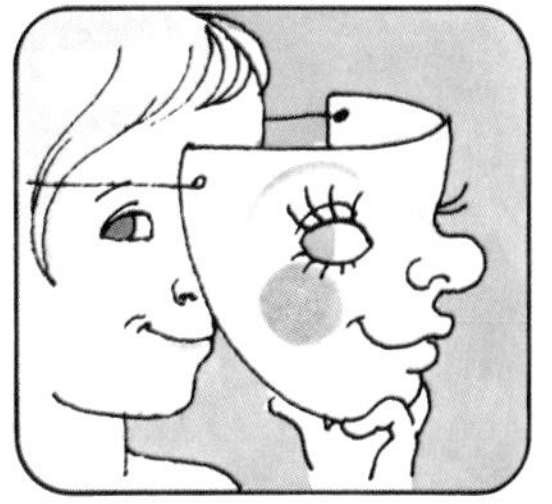

mask

matches

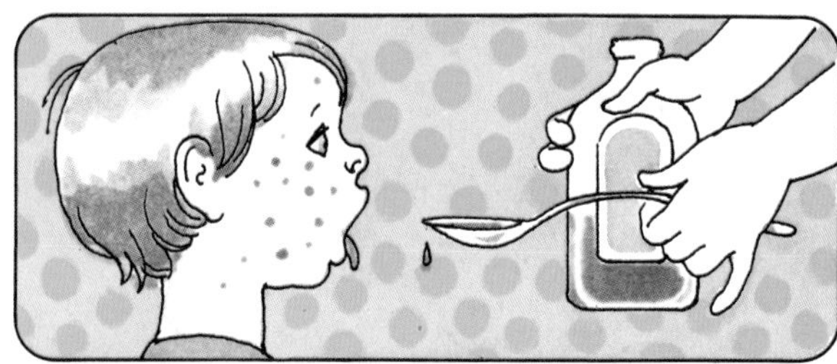

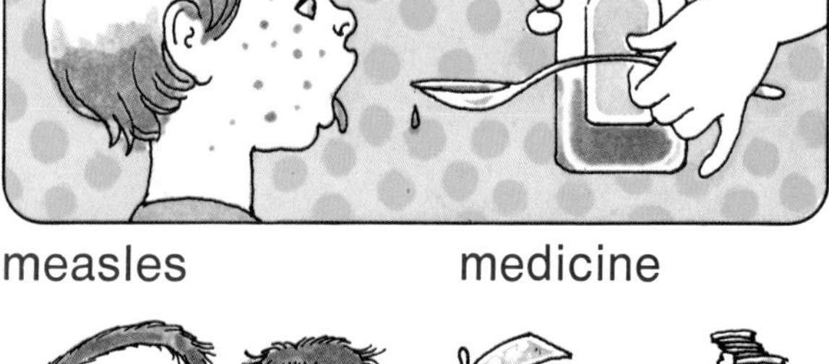

measles medicine

mittens

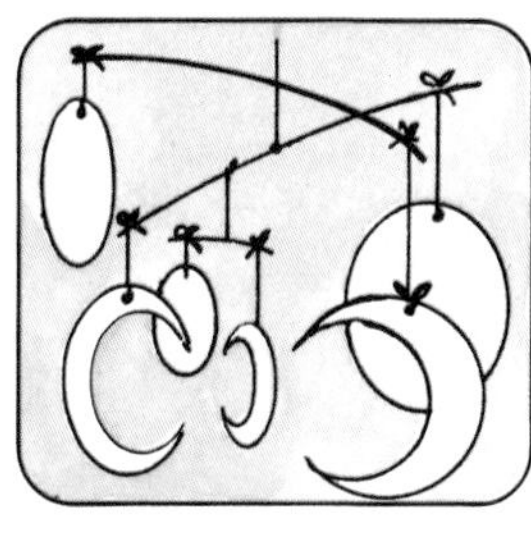

mobile

monkey money

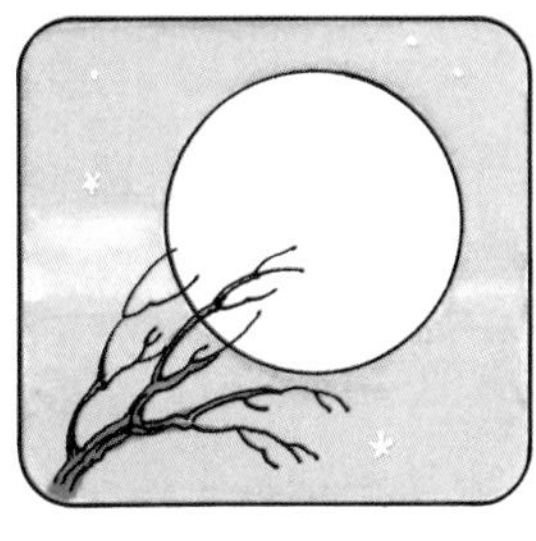

moon

motorbike

mouse

mumps

How many more m words do you know?

abcdefghijkl **m** nopqrstuvwxyz

M
m

machines

Machines help us do work. Many machines have wheels. Can you find the wheels on these machines?

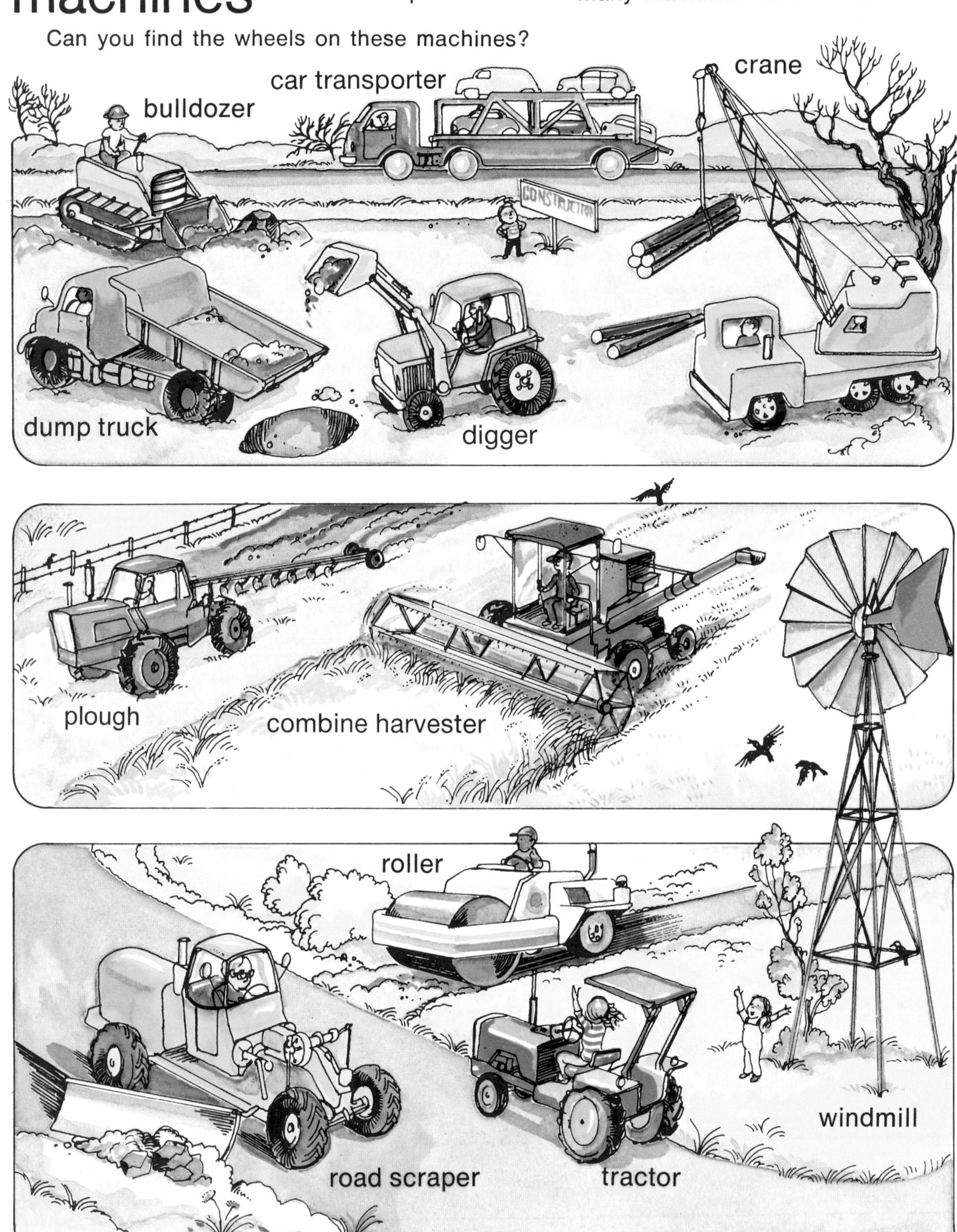

mountain

Mountains are very high hills.
They are made of rock.
Some people live on mountains.

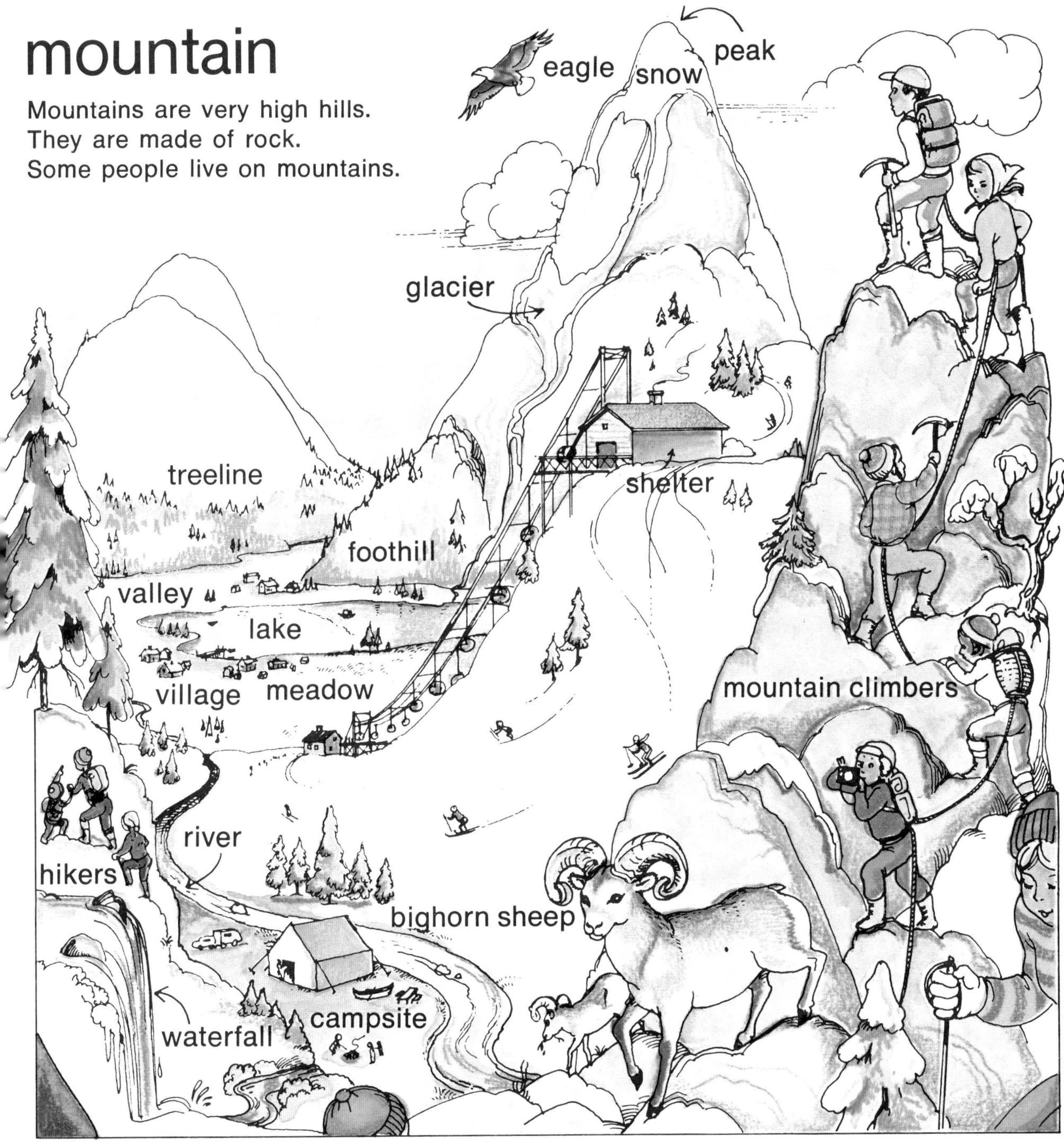

eagle
snow
peak
glacier
treeline
shelter
foothill
valley
lake
village
meadow
mountain climbers
hikers
river
bighorn sheep
campsite
waterfall

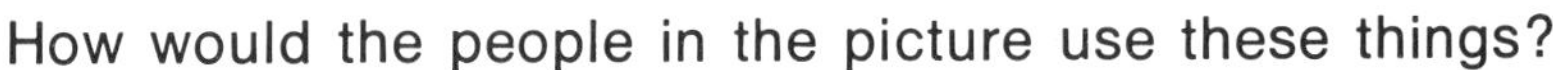

How would the people in the picture use these things?

rucksack
pickaxe
ski pole
rope
skis
boot

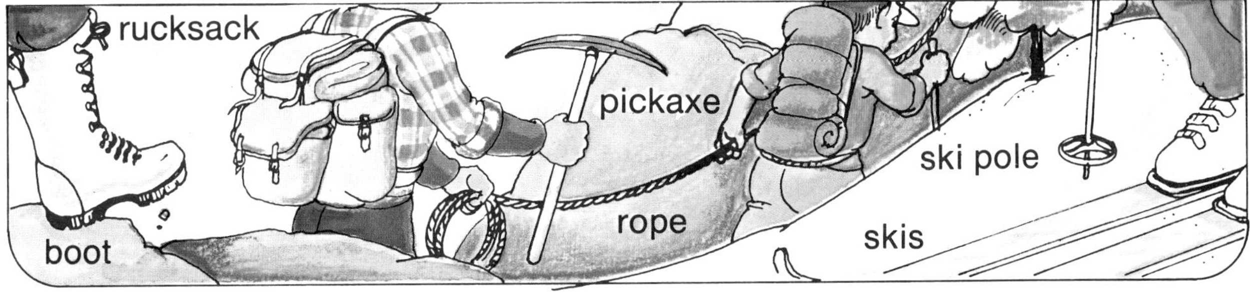

M
m

museums

Many wonderful things are cared for in museums. We can go there to see them.

The things we see in museums are called exhibits.
Which exhibit do you like best?

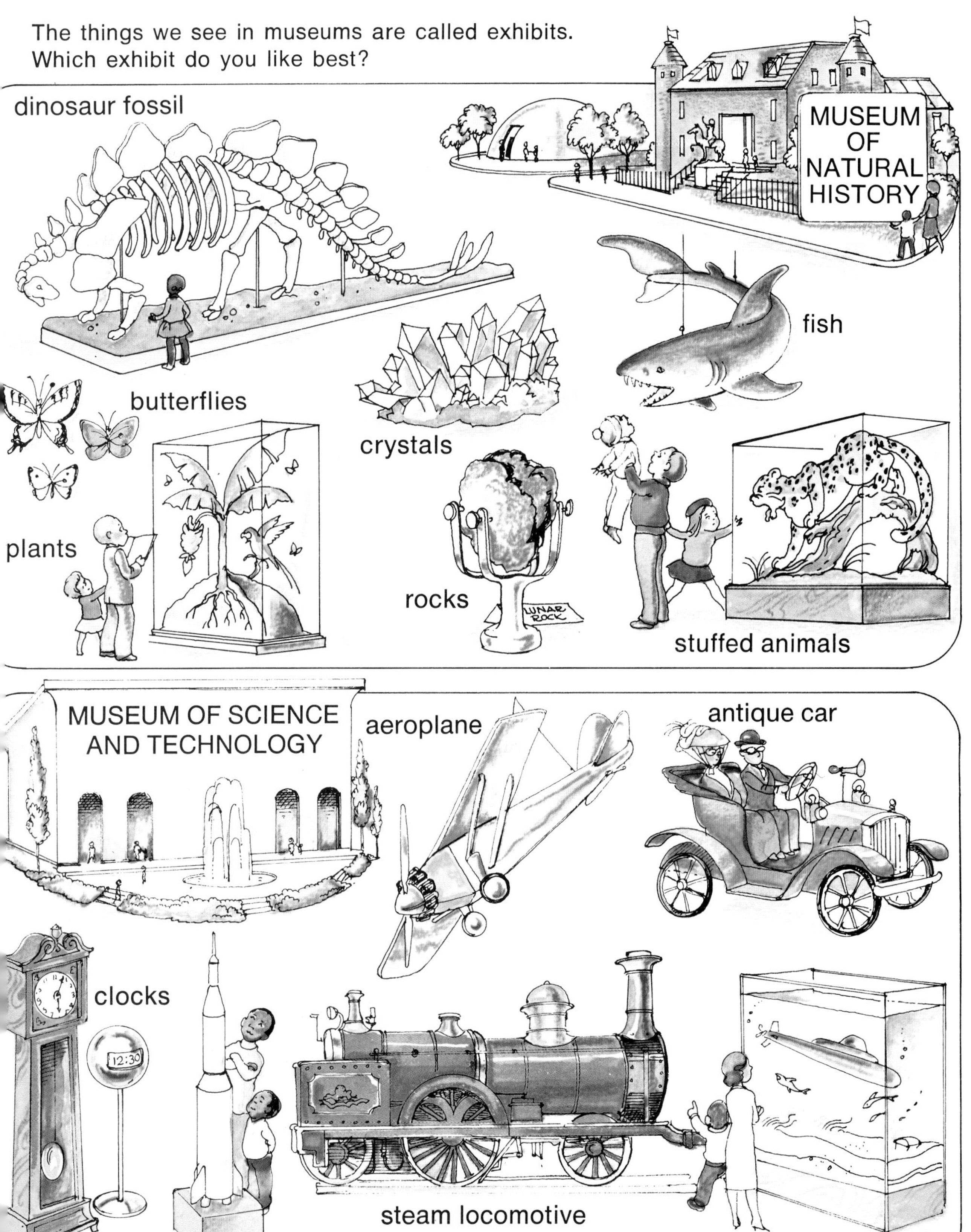

M
m

music

Do you like to listen to music?
These musicians enjoy playing together.

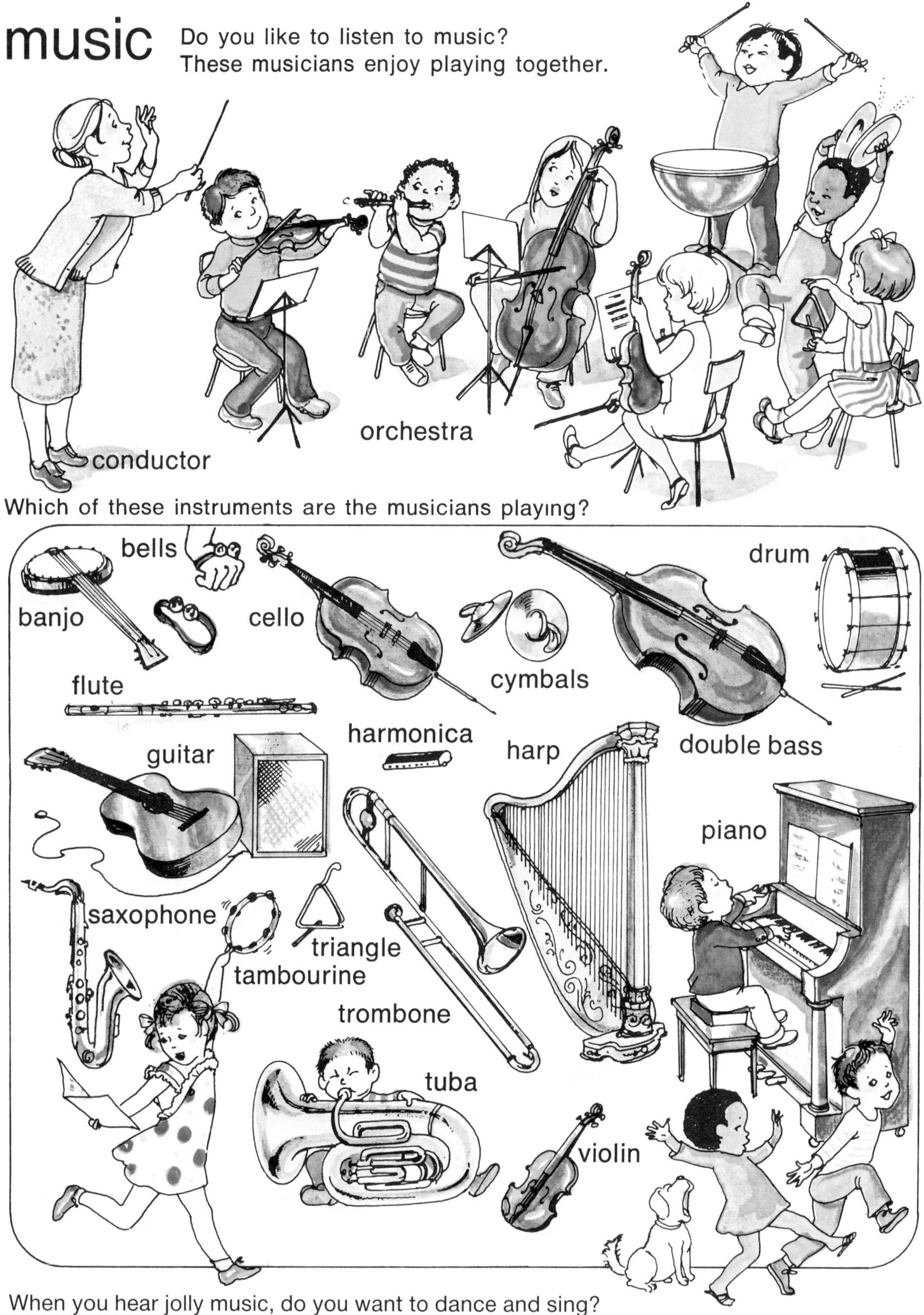

Which of these instruments are the musicians playing?

When you hear jolly music, do you want to dance and sing?

Nancy needs a nap.

ABCDEFGHIJKLM  OPQRSTUVWXYZ

The names of these objects begin with N.

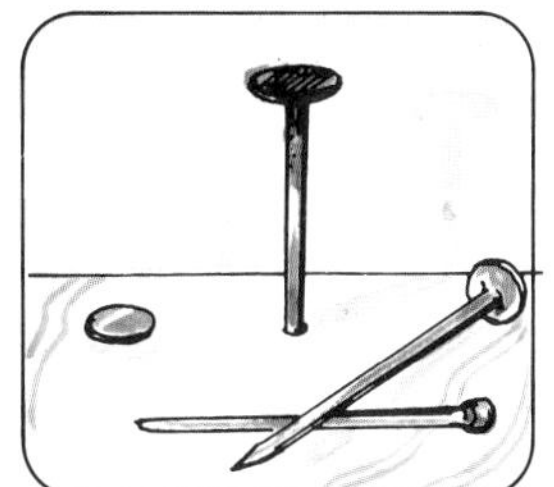

nails

napkin

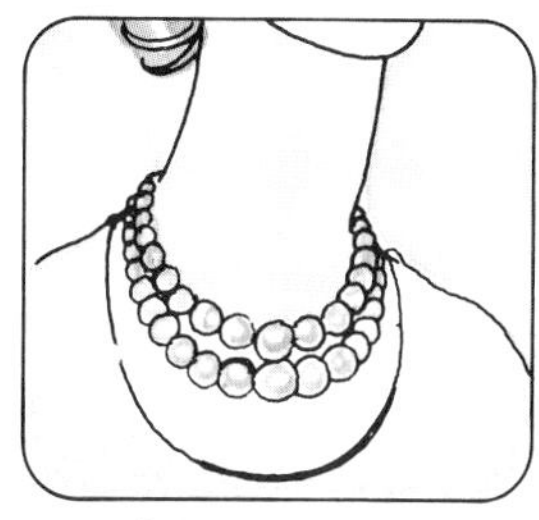

necklace

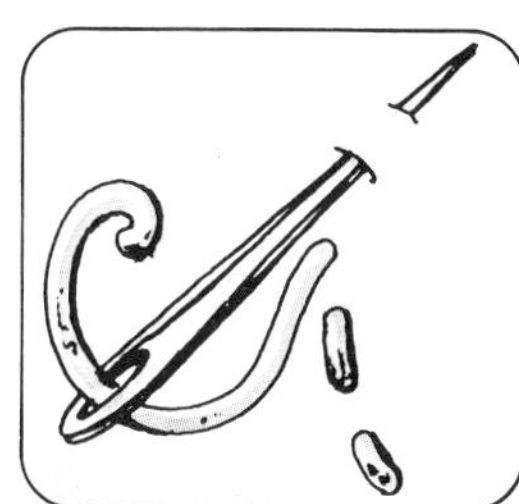

needle

nest

net

newspaper

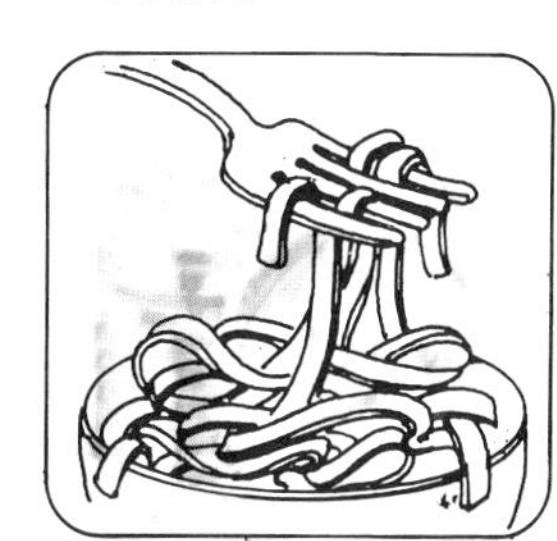

noodles

notebook

nutcracker

nuts

Can you think of nine nice new n words?

abcdefghijklm  opqrstuvwxyz

N
n

names

We have names so people will know who we are.
What is your name?

numbers

Numbers tell us how many.

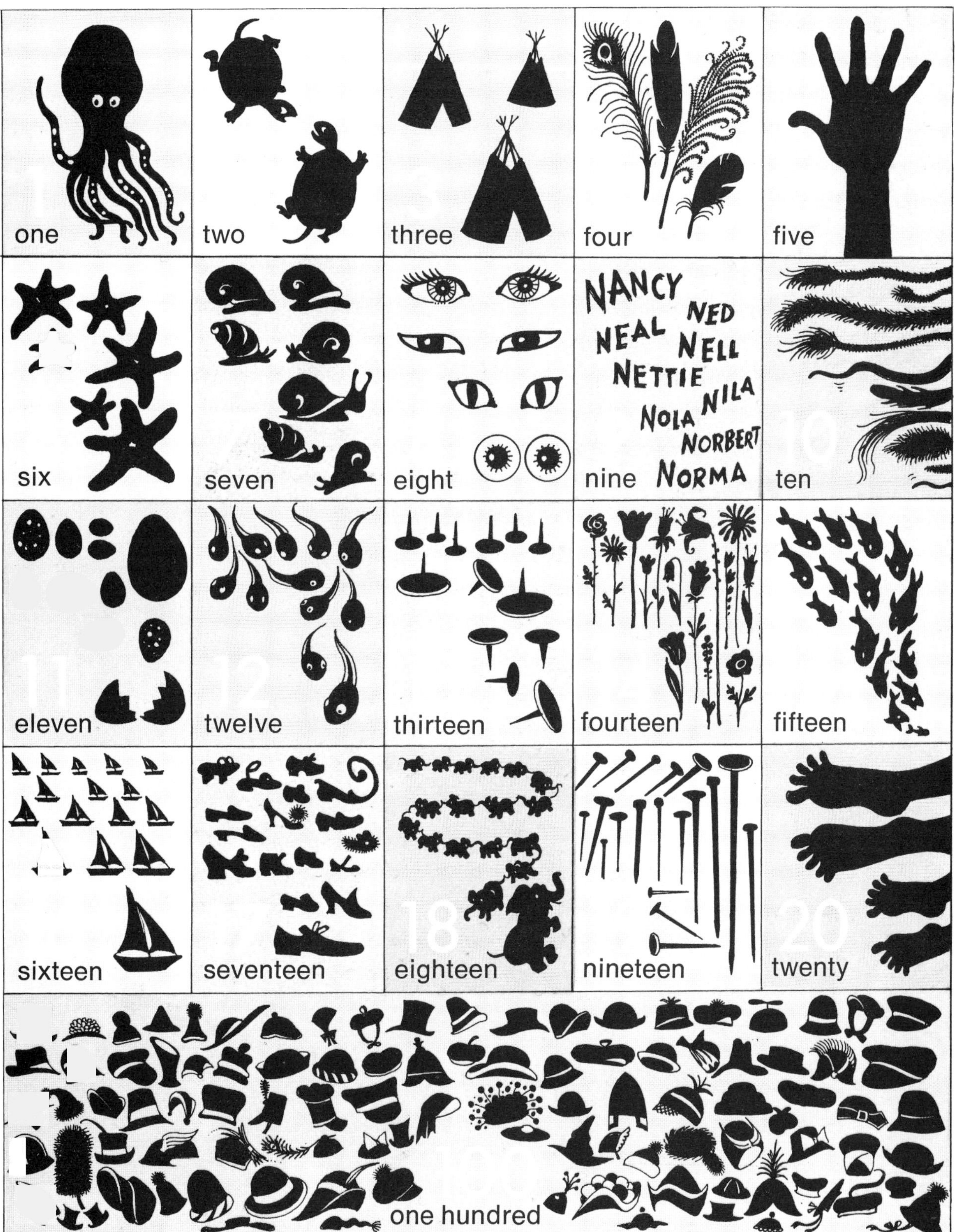

Oliver owns an octopus.

ABCDEFGHIJKLMN  PQRSTUVWXYZ

These words start with O.

oboe

oilcan

olive

one onion

orange

organ

ostrich

otter

overalls

owl

ox

oyster

Can you think of some other O words?

a b c d e f g h i j k l m n 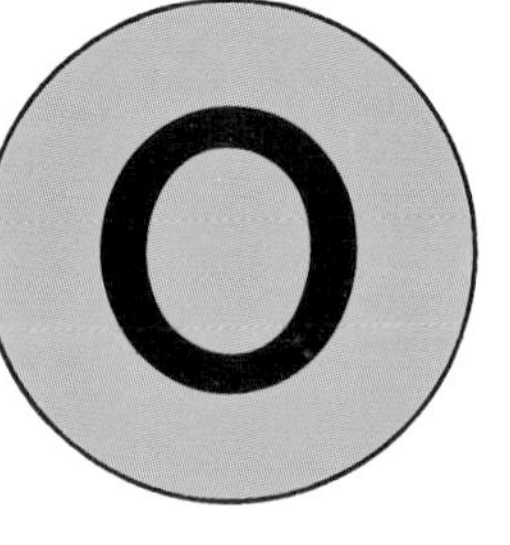 p q r s t u v w x y z

ocean

The oceans cover most of the Earth. They are filled with salt water.

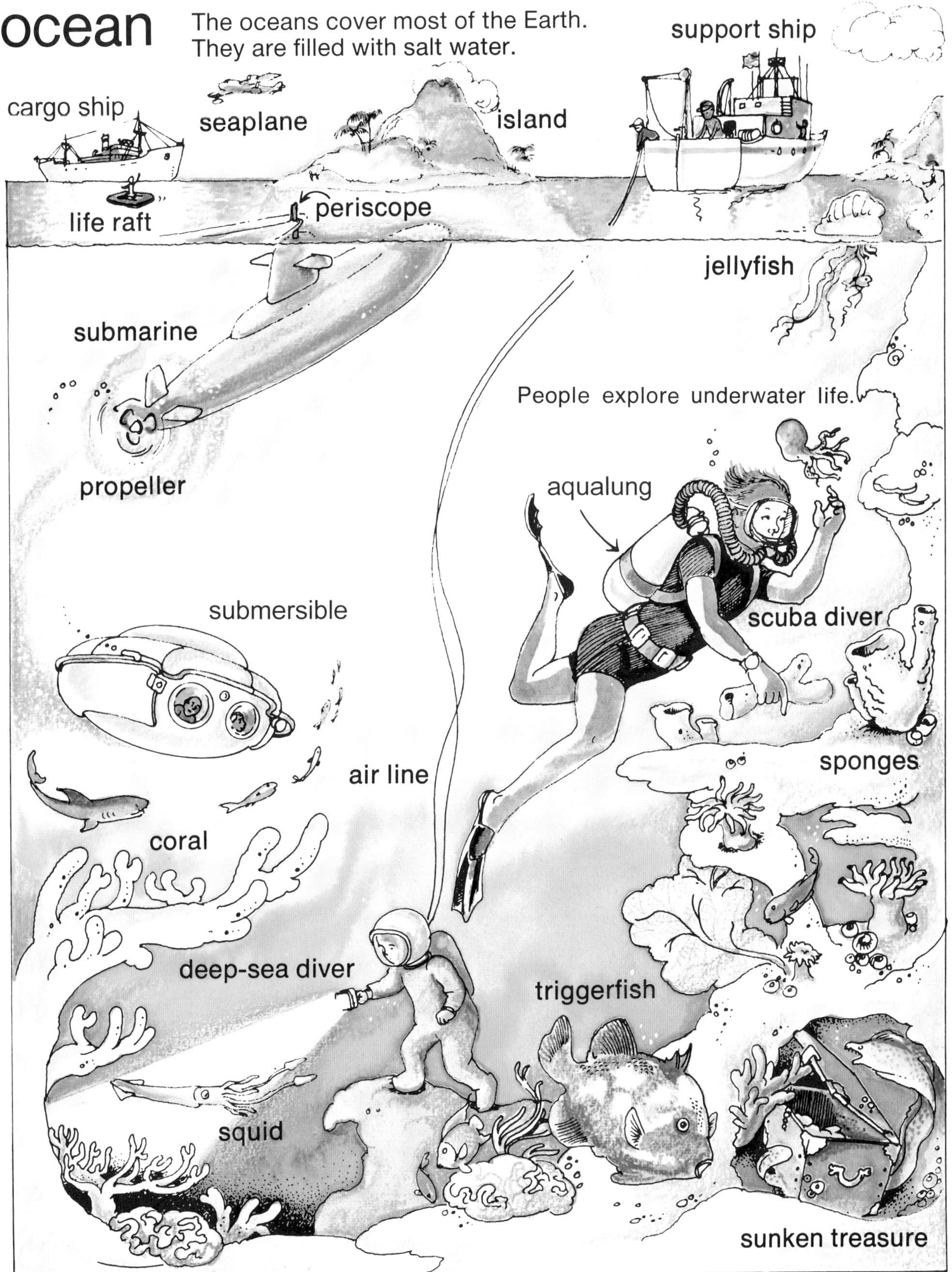

O
o

opposites

When things are altogether different, we say that they are opposite each other.

up

down

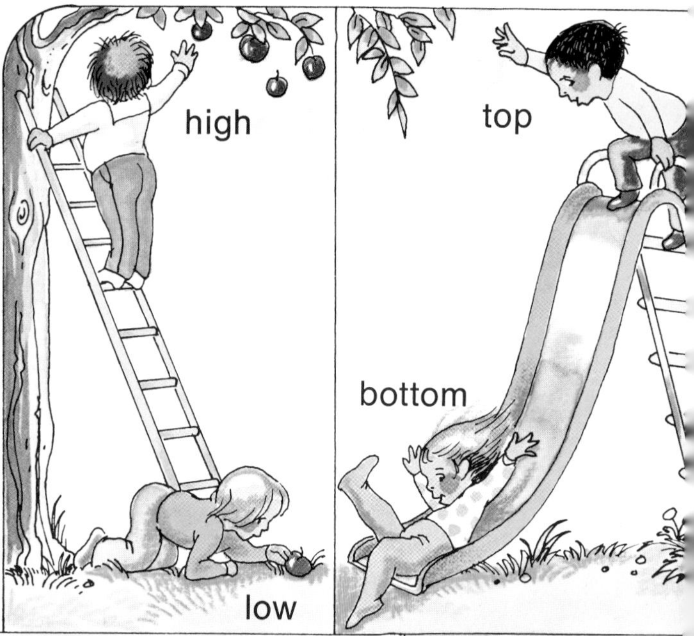

high

low

top

bottom

on

off

over

under

inside

outside

upside down

right side up

left

right

push

pull

old
new
happy
sad
asleep
awake
stop
go
tall
short
fat
thin
ENTRANCE
EXIT
KINDER-
GARTEN
HELLO
GOOD BYE
in
out
come
go

Pamela pets her puppy.

ABCDEFGHIJKLMNO **P** QRSTUVWXYZ

The words on this page begin with the letter P.

pans

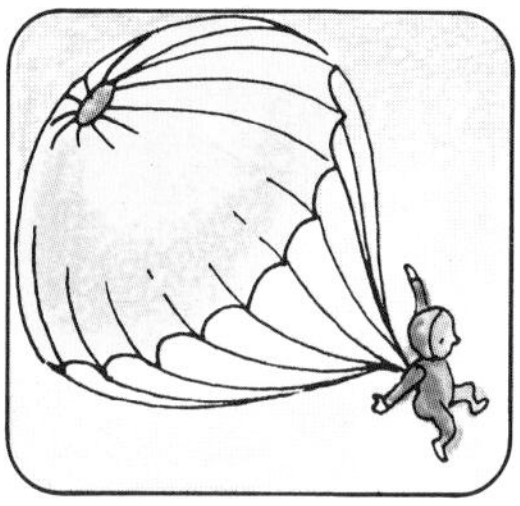

parachute

paste

peacock

peanut

pelican

penknife

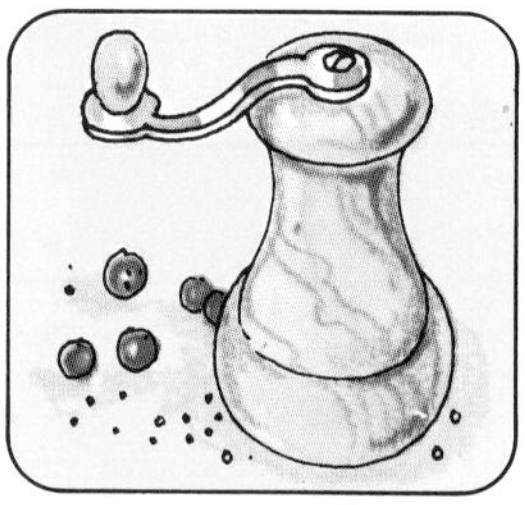

pepper

pink pig

pizza

pitcher

porpoise

Can you pick out some words that have the letter p in the middle?

abcdefghijklmno **p** qrstuvwxyz

park

People like to go to the park to relax and play.

Pam and Penny are playing hopscotch.
Paul and Peter are playing tag.
What are the other people doing?

What do you like to do in the park?

P
p

pets

Pets are special animal friends.

Which of these pets would you like for your friend?

canary

cat

fish

budgerigar

mouse

hamster

dog

gerbil

pony

snake

turtle

Which of these things would you use to take care of the pets you chose?

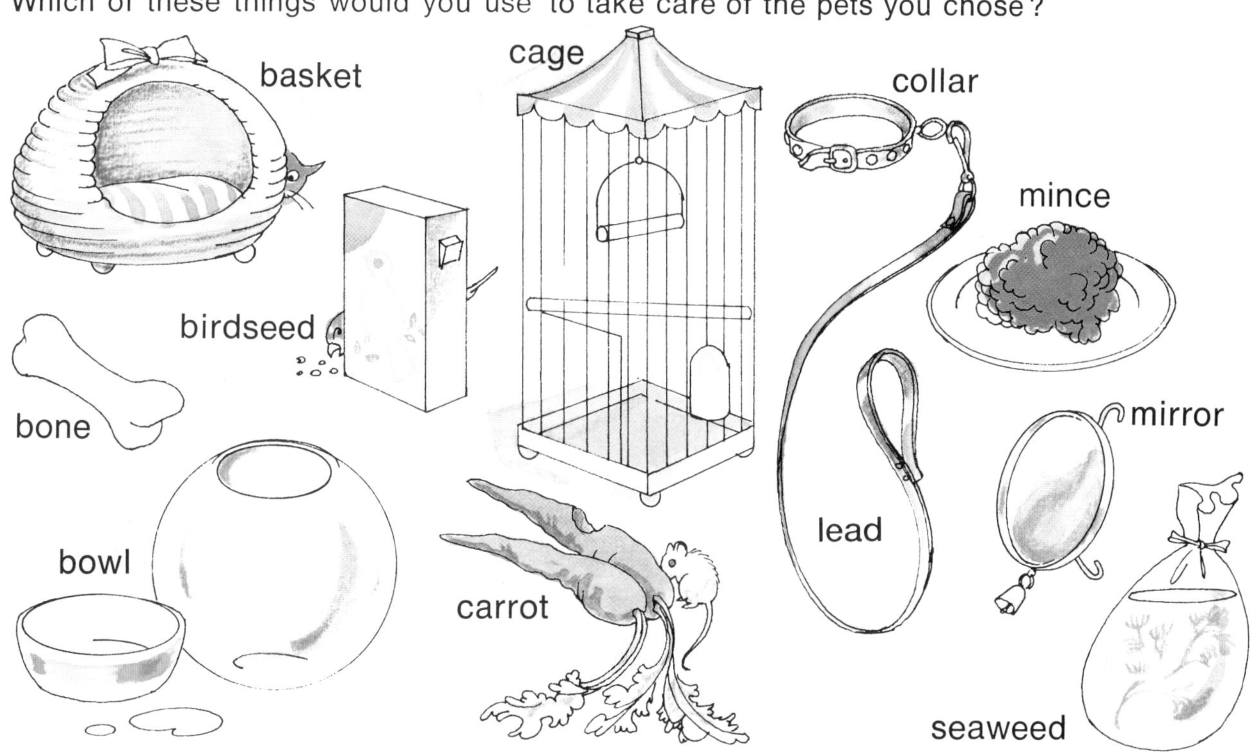

P
p

plants

There are many kinds of plants in the world. They are different shapes and different sizes.

Trees are the biggest plants.

Some plants are so tiny that we need a microscope to see them.

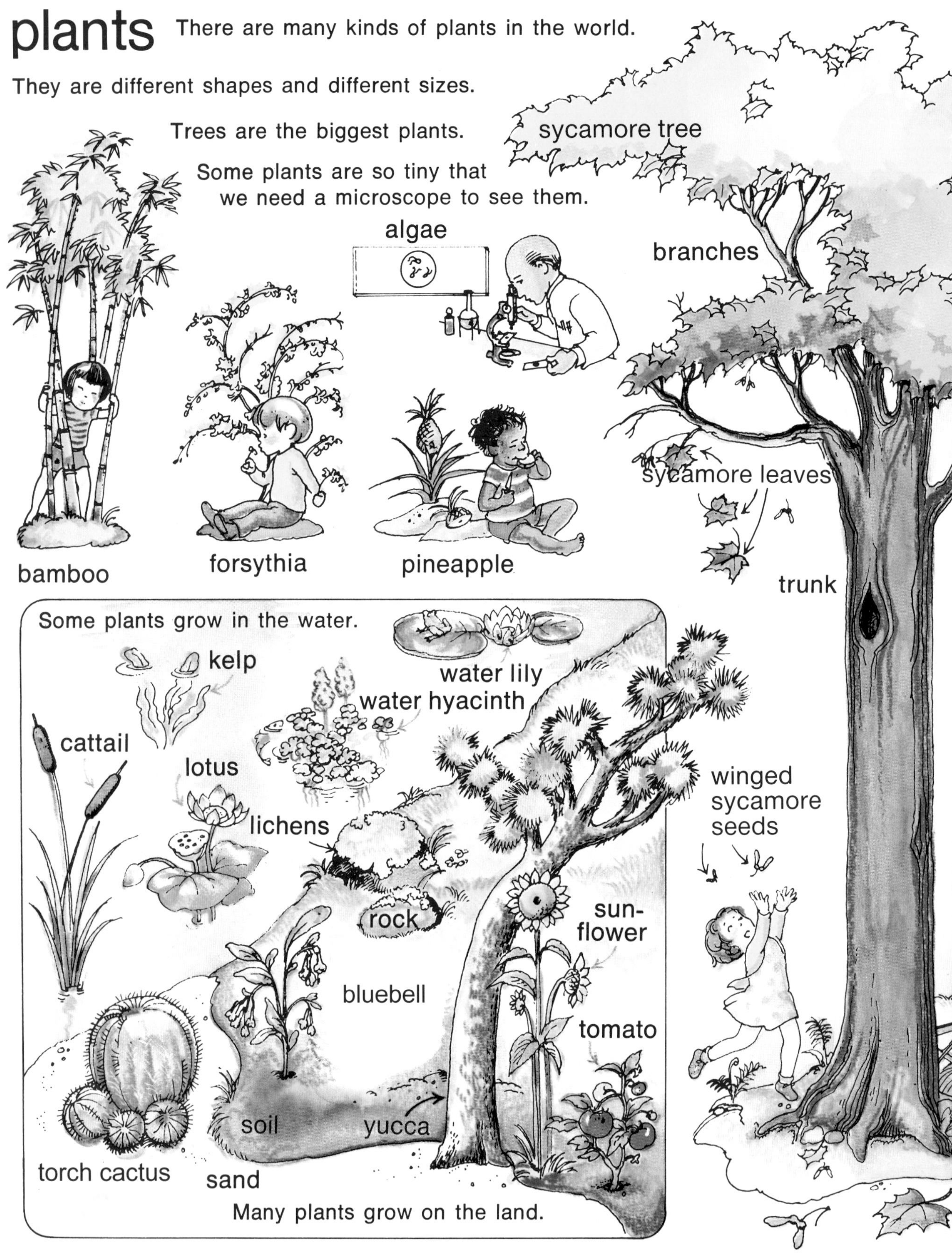

Most plants are green.
Sunshine helps them manufacture their own food.

Some plants are not green.
They get their food from other plants.

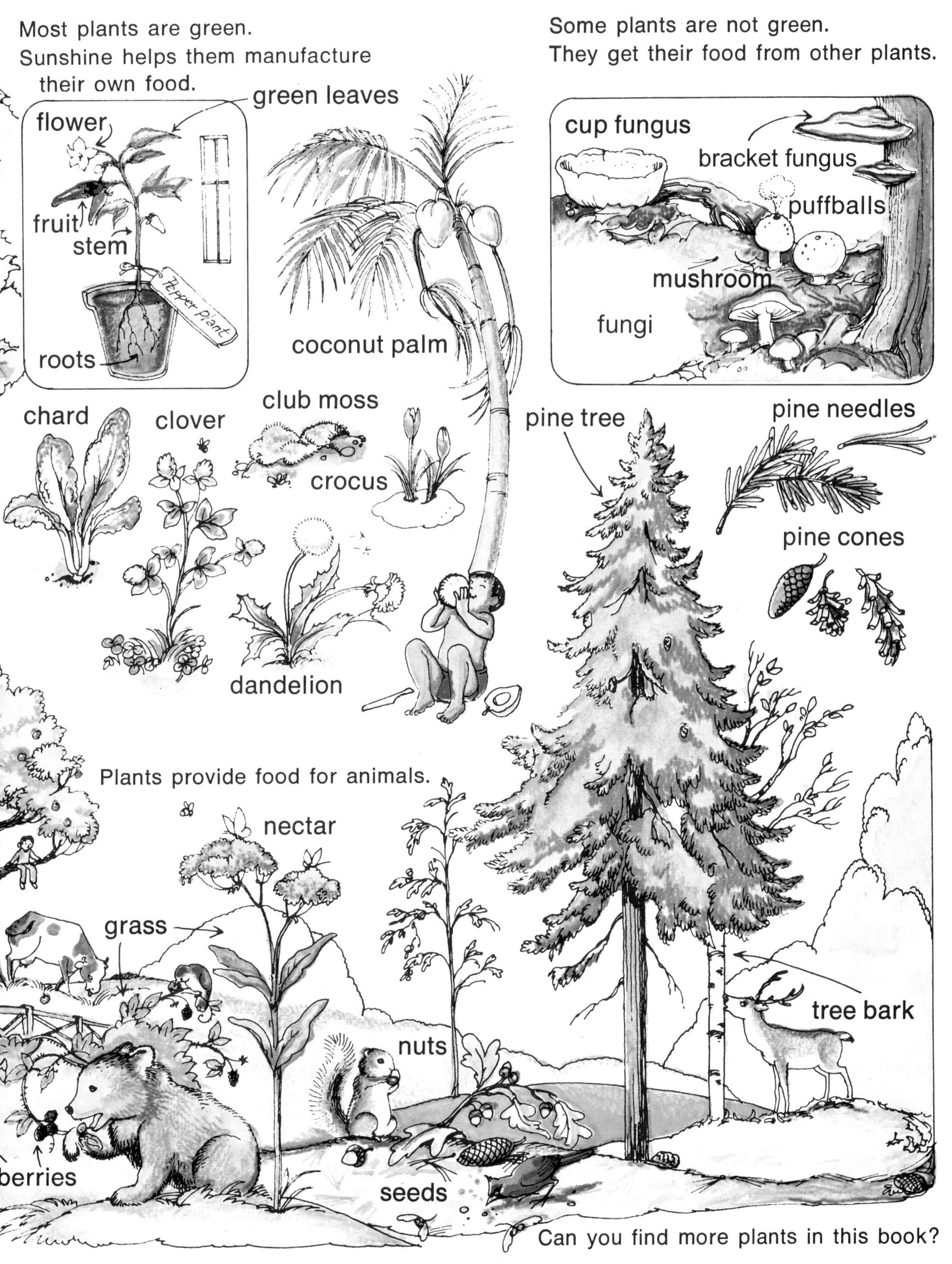

Plants provide food for animals.

Can you find more plants in this book?

Quentin quarters a quince.

ABCDEFGHIJKLMNOP Q RSTUVWXYZ

These words begin with Q.

quail

quarry

queen questions

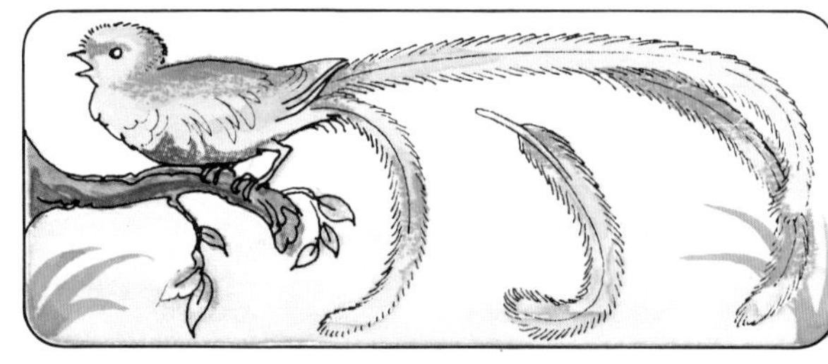

quetzal quill

quilt

quiver

quoits

Did you notice that q is always followed by U?

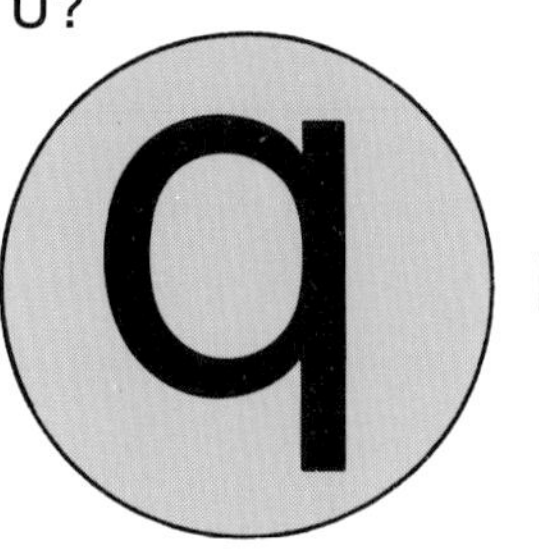

abcdefghijklmnop q rstuvwxyz

Ruth rides in a rowing boat on the river.

ABCDEFGHIJKLMNOPQ R STUVWXYZ

Can you read these words that begin with R?

raccoon	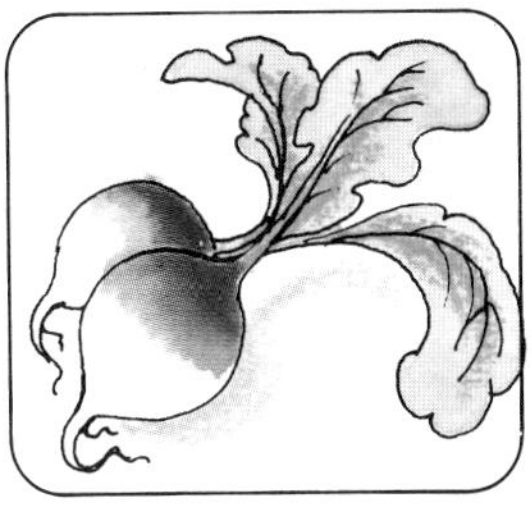 radish	 raisins	 rake
 record	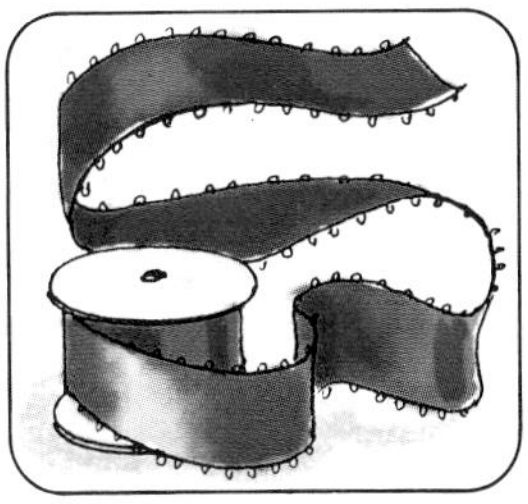 red ribbon	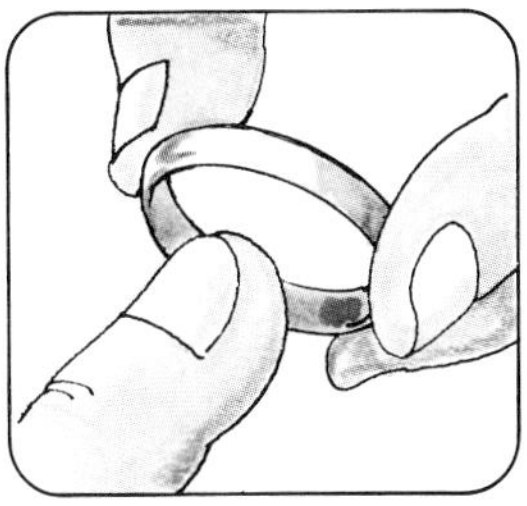 ring	 rooster
 rope	 rose	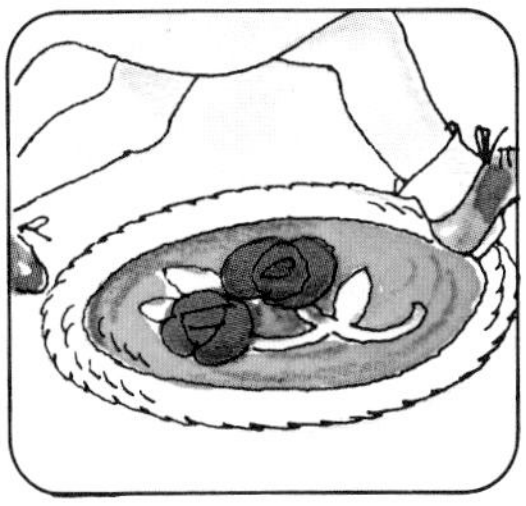 rug	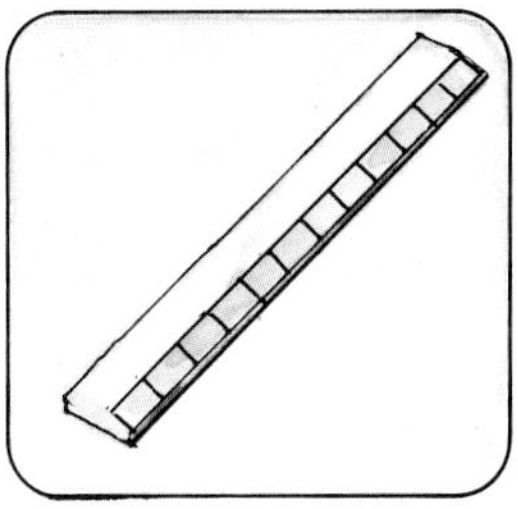 ruler

Which of the words end with r?

a b c d e f g h i j k l m n o p q  s t u v w x y z

R
r

ranch

Some large farms in America are called ranches. Ranchers raise cattle and horses.

windmill
water hole
ranch house
rancher
Would you like to compete at a rodeo?
Rodeo Today
riding a wild horse
jumping from horse to horse
roping steers
rope tricks
shooting contest

R
r

river

A river is a large stream of water that flows to the sea.

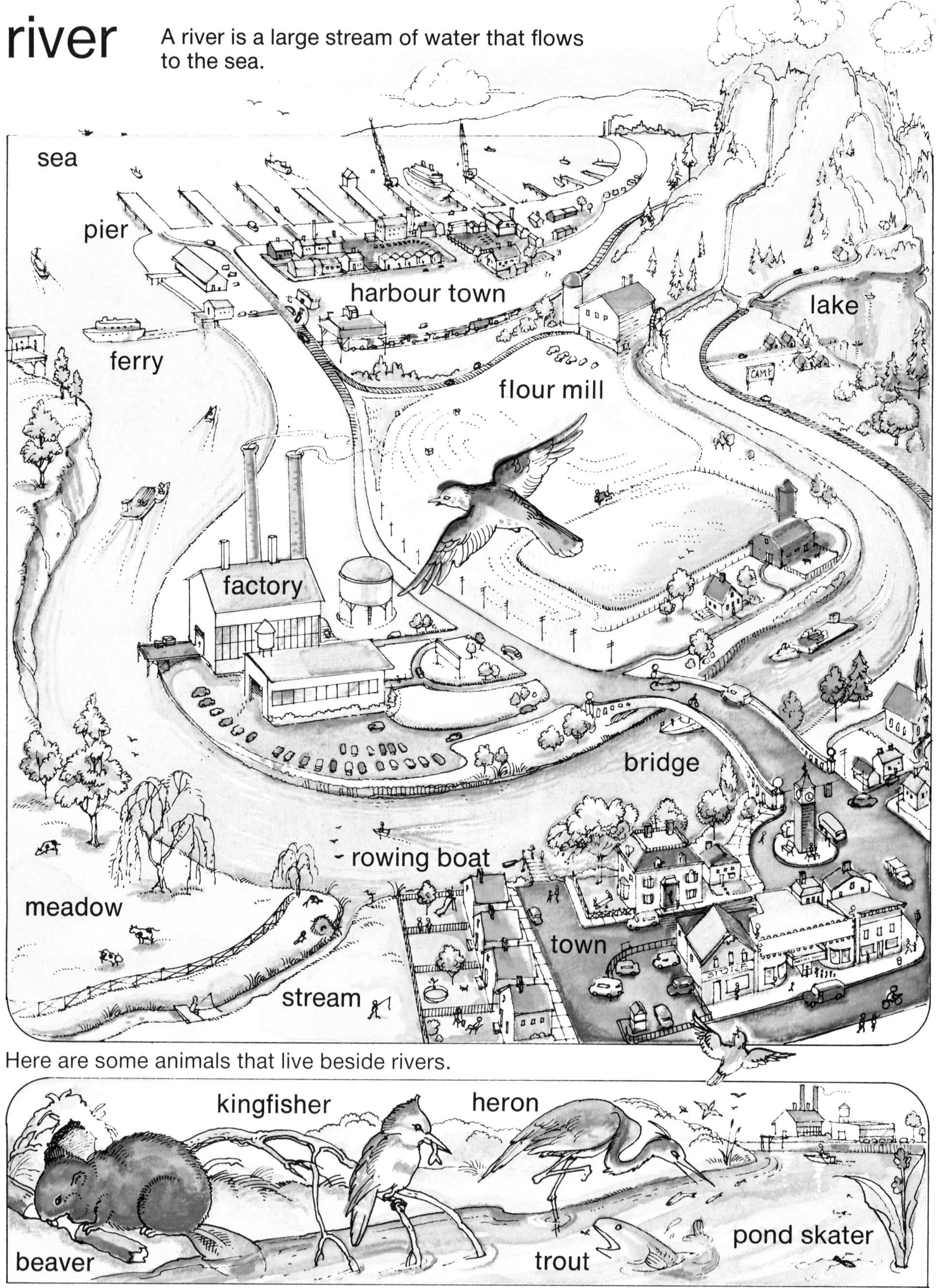

Here are some animals that live beside rivers.

Sam sings a silly song.

ABCDEFGHIJKLMNOPQR  TUVWXYZ

See all the words that start with S.

safe

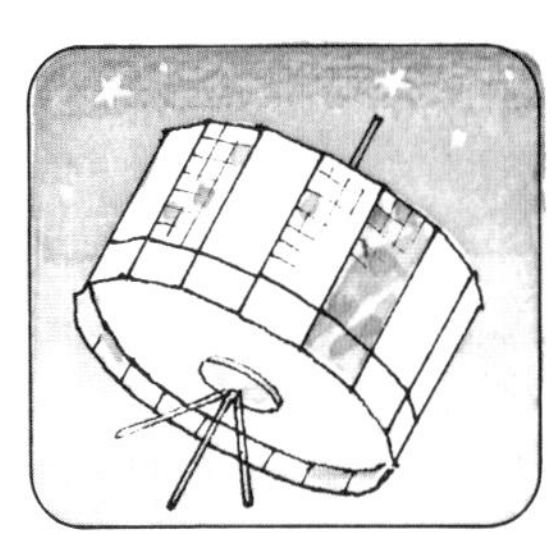

satellite

seven seashells

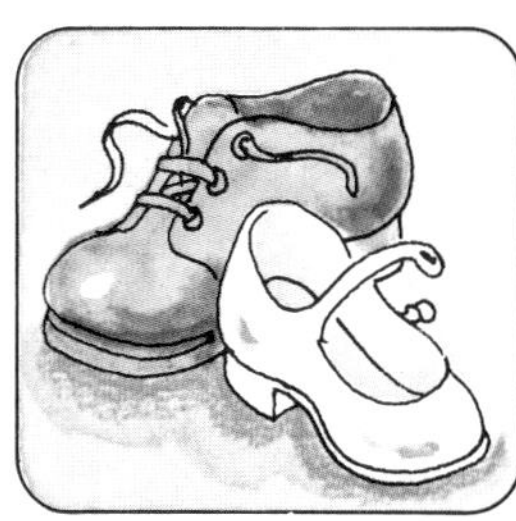

shoes

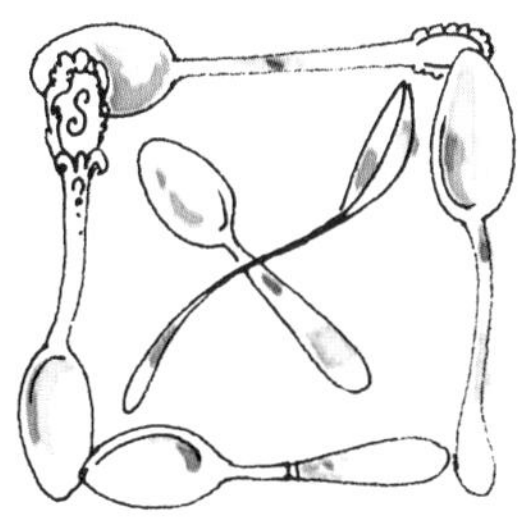

six spoons

skeleton skunk

snowman

snowmobile stagecoach

string

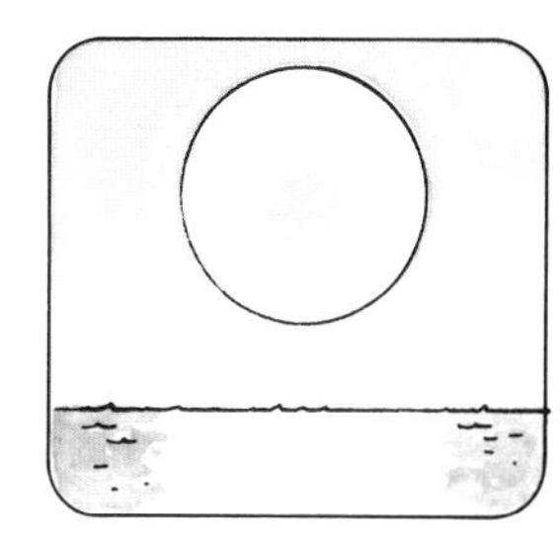

sun

Can you think of several more S words?

abcdefghijklmnopqr  tuvwxyz

seashore

Land by the sea is called the seashore.

Which of these things would you take to the beach?

beach bag
beach ball
life jacket
bucket
spade
chair
sunglasses
towel
toy
sieve
swimming trunks
umbrella

S
s

Have you ever seen these animals at the seashore?

seasons

There are four seasons in each year.
In many parts of the world the weather changes with the seasons.

What do you do each season of the year?

shapes

You can cut paper into different shapes.

S
s

sports

Sports are games people play for recreation.

Which are indoor sports? Which are outdoor sports?

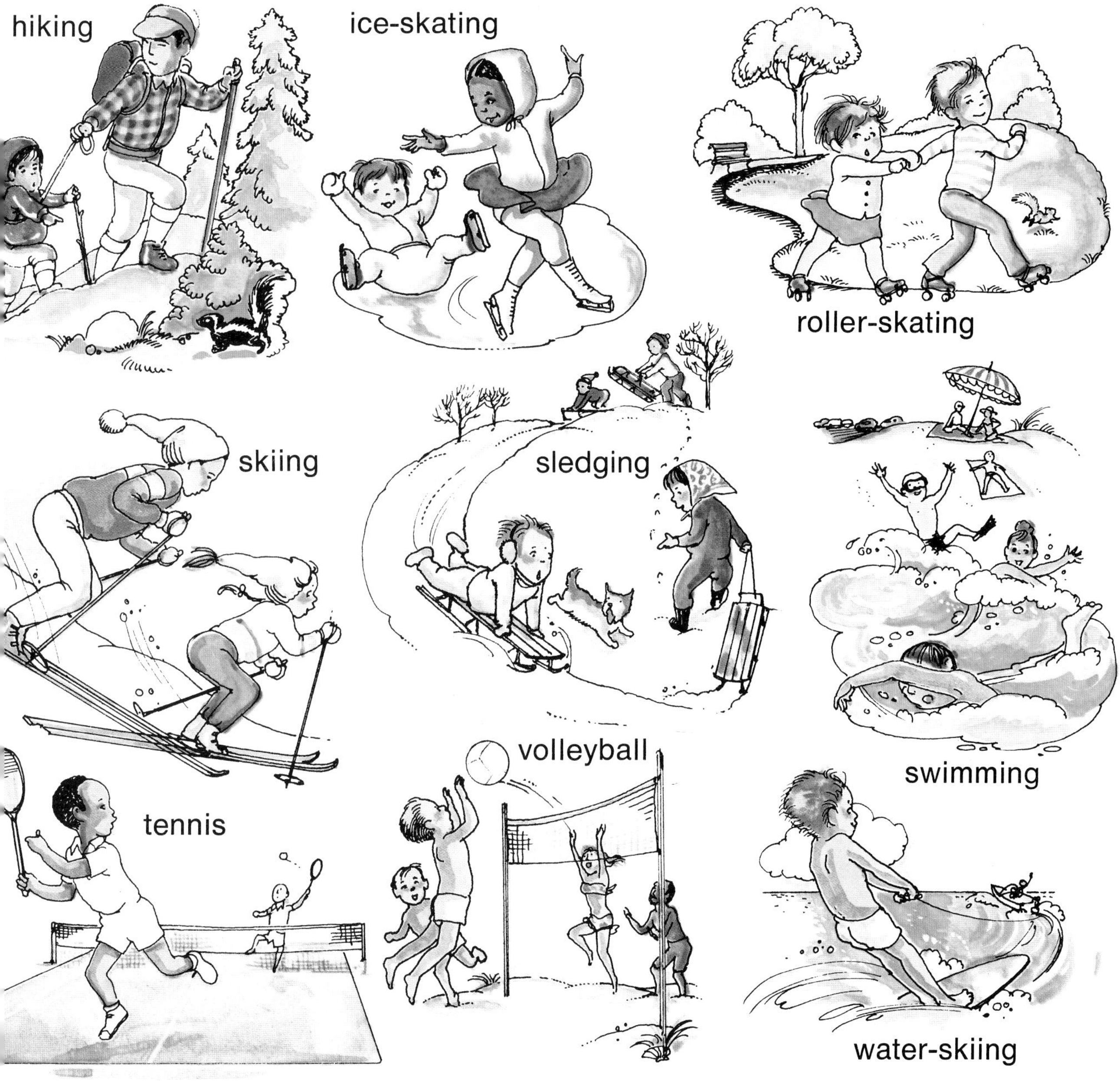

hiking
ice-skating
roller-skating
skiing
sledging
swimming
tennis
volleyball
water-skiing

How do the players use these objects?

bat
bow and arrow
croquet mallet
cricket bat
mask
golf club
fishing rod
ski poles
tennis
racket

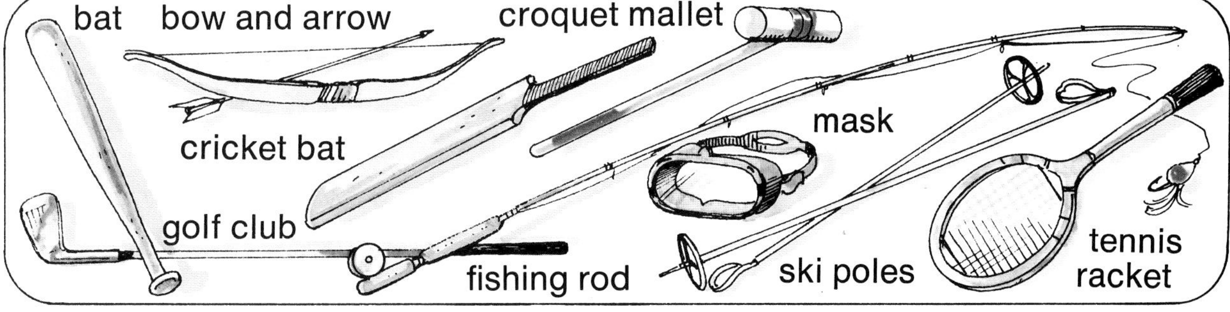

Tom talks on the telephone.

ABCDEFGHIJKLMNOPQRS

UVWXYZ

These words start with T.

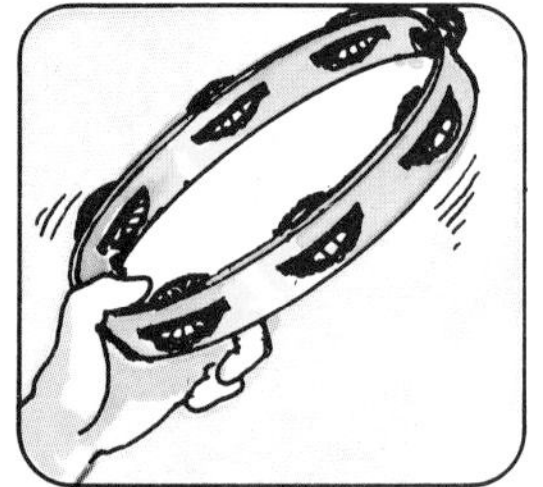

tambourine

taxi

television

ten triangles

three thimbles

tickets

tired turtle

toboggan

toy train

trunk

two tall trees

twins

Does it tickle your tongue to say t words?

abcdefghijklmnopqrs

uvwxyz

time

Clocks and watches help us tell time.

minute hand

hour hand

cuckoo clock

alarm clock

grandfather clock

electric clock

pocket watch

wristwatch

Here are some other things that help us keep track of time.

What time do you do these things?

T
t

tools

We use tools to help us get work done.

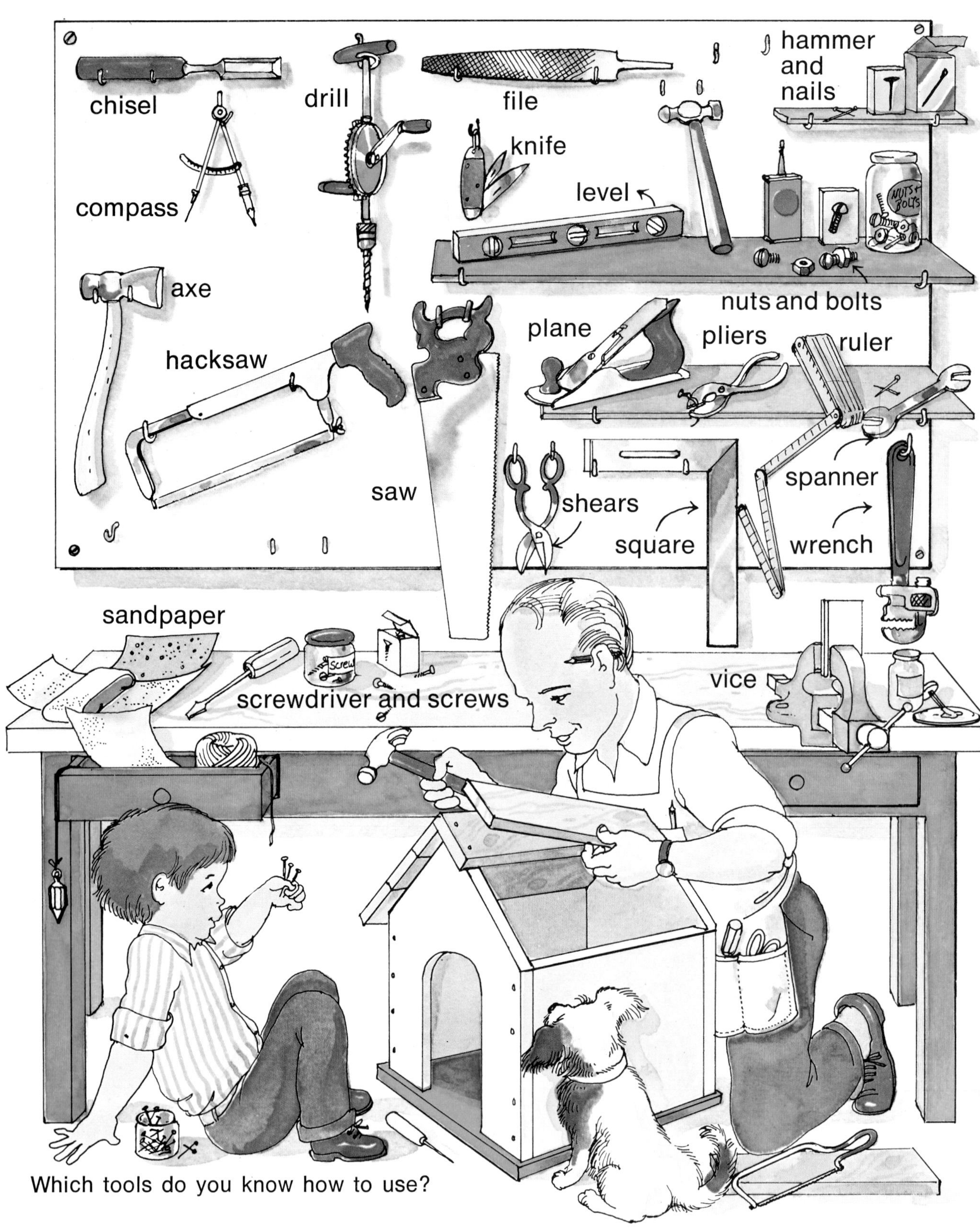

Which tools do you know how to use?

toys

Things we play with are called toys.
Which toys would you like to play with?

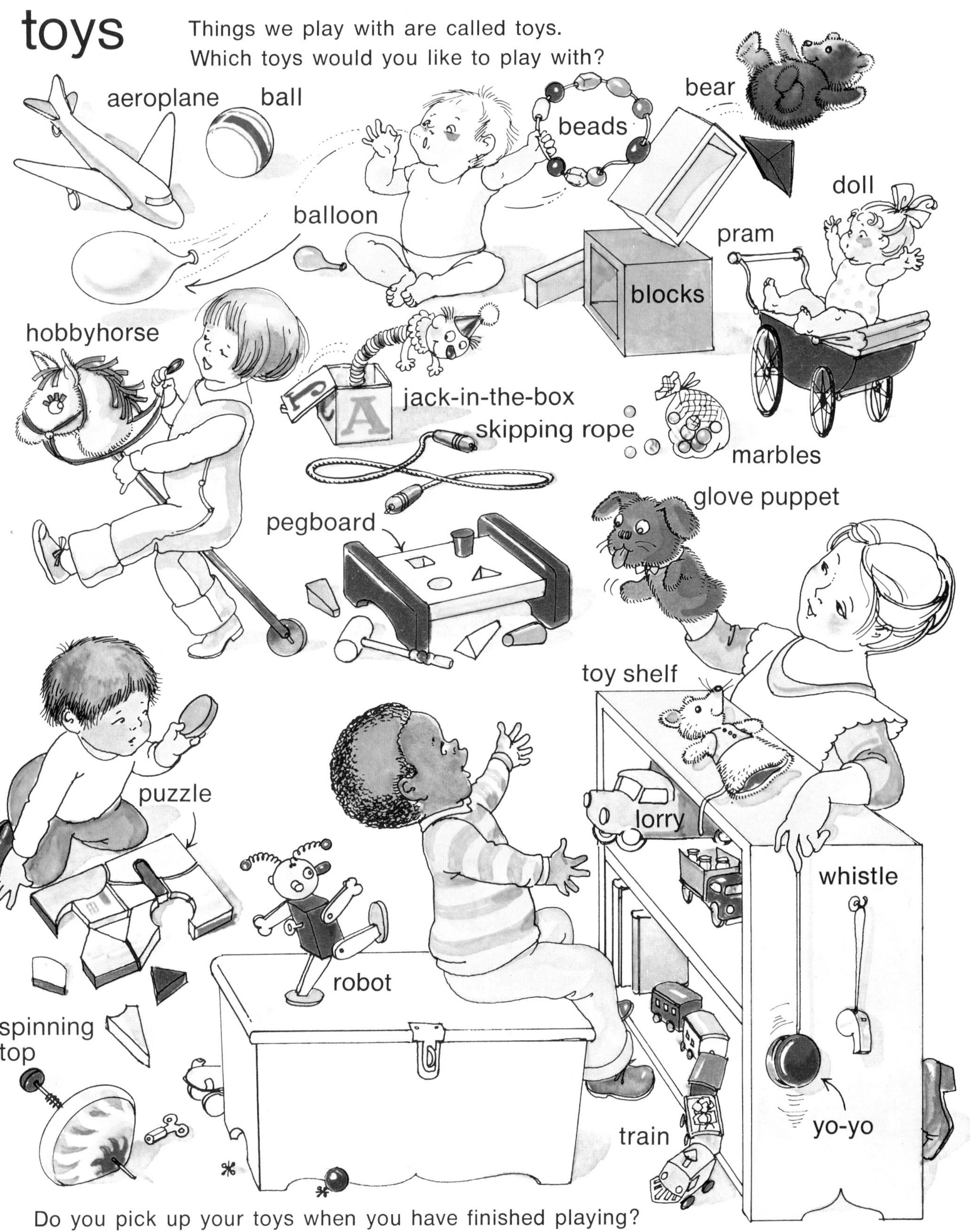

Do you pick up your toys when you have finished playing?

T
t

transportation

'Transportation' means carrying people and things from place to place.

Find different ways of travelling on land.

Find different ways of travelling through the air.

Find different ways of travelling on the water.

airship
aeroplane
seaplane
ocean liner
sailing boat
bridge
lorry
tollbooth
tunnel
taxi
carriages
tugboat
train
gine
barge

Ursula uses her umbrella.

ABCDEFGHIJKLMNOPQRST

VWXYZ

Here are some words that begin with U.

ukulele

umbrella

umpire

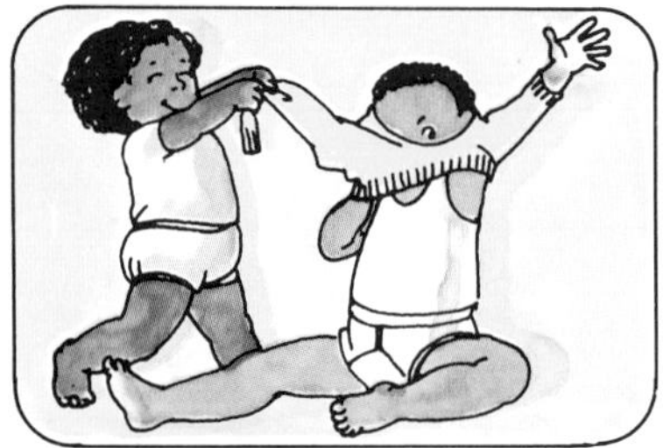

underwear

unicorn

unicycle

United Nations

United States of America

upside down

Can you tell a story using these u words?

abcdefghijklmnopqrst

vwxyz

underground

Many things are happening underground.

Here are some of the things we usually cannot see.

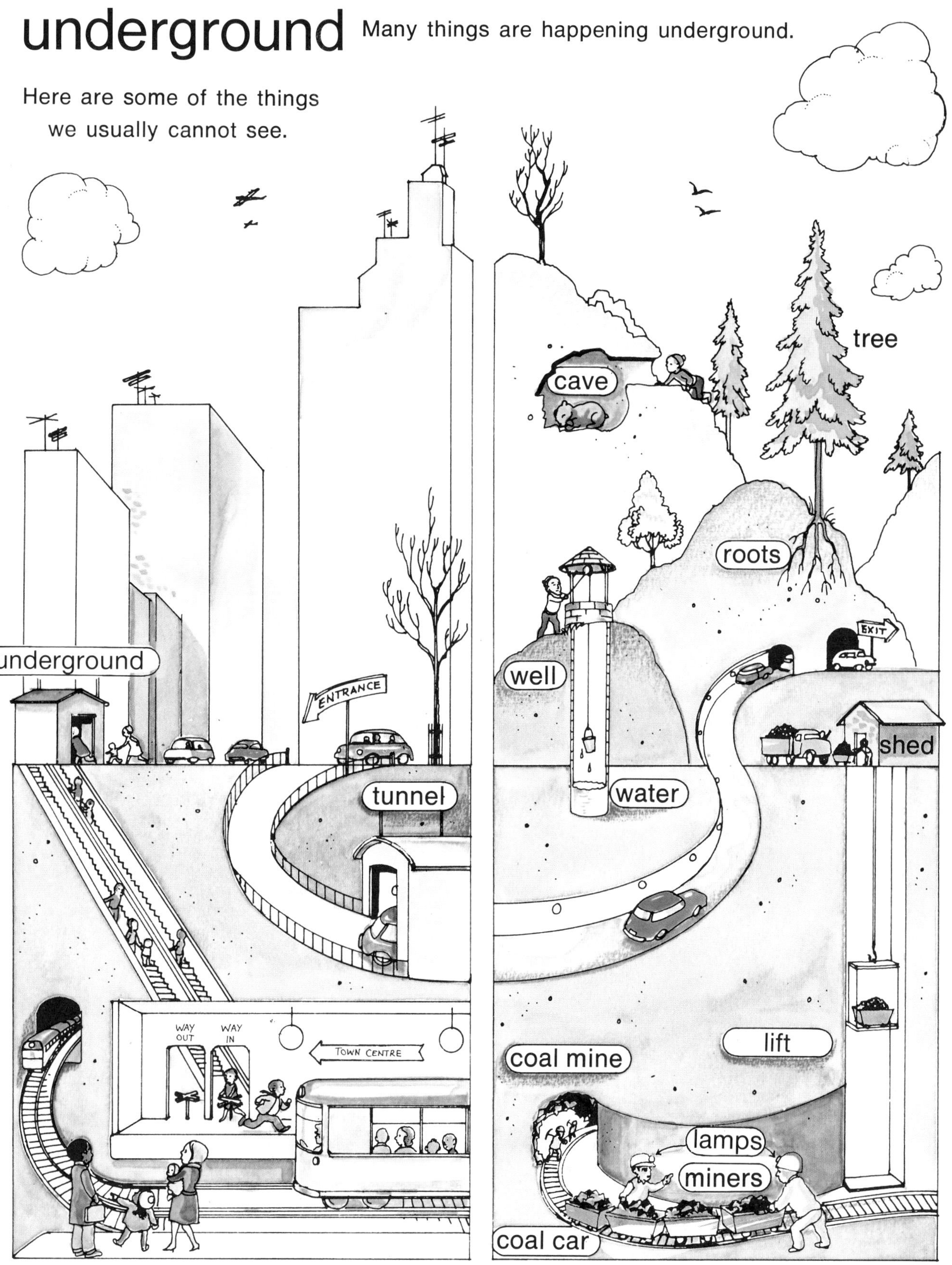

Victor visits Venice.

ABCDEFGHIJKLMNOPQRSTU  WXYZ

There aren't very many words that start with V.

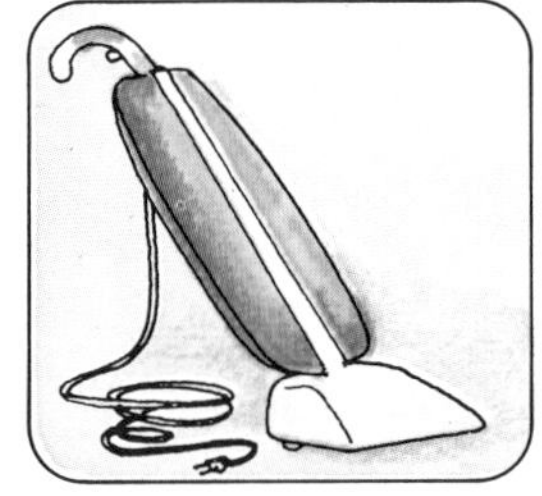

vacuum cleaner

valentine

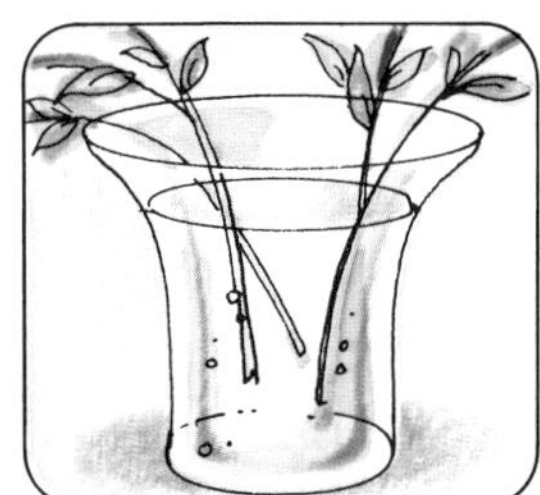

vase

vine

violets

violin

vice

vitamins

volcano

volleyball

vulture

Can you think of any more V words?

abcdefghijklmnopqrstu 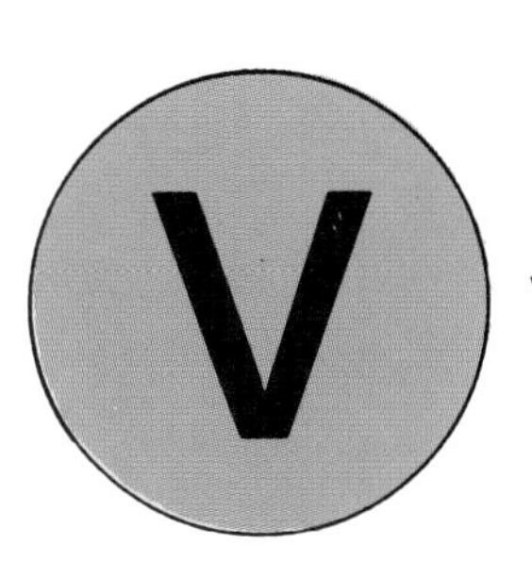 wxyz

vegetables

Vegetables are parts of plants we use for food.

Sometimes we eat the leaves.

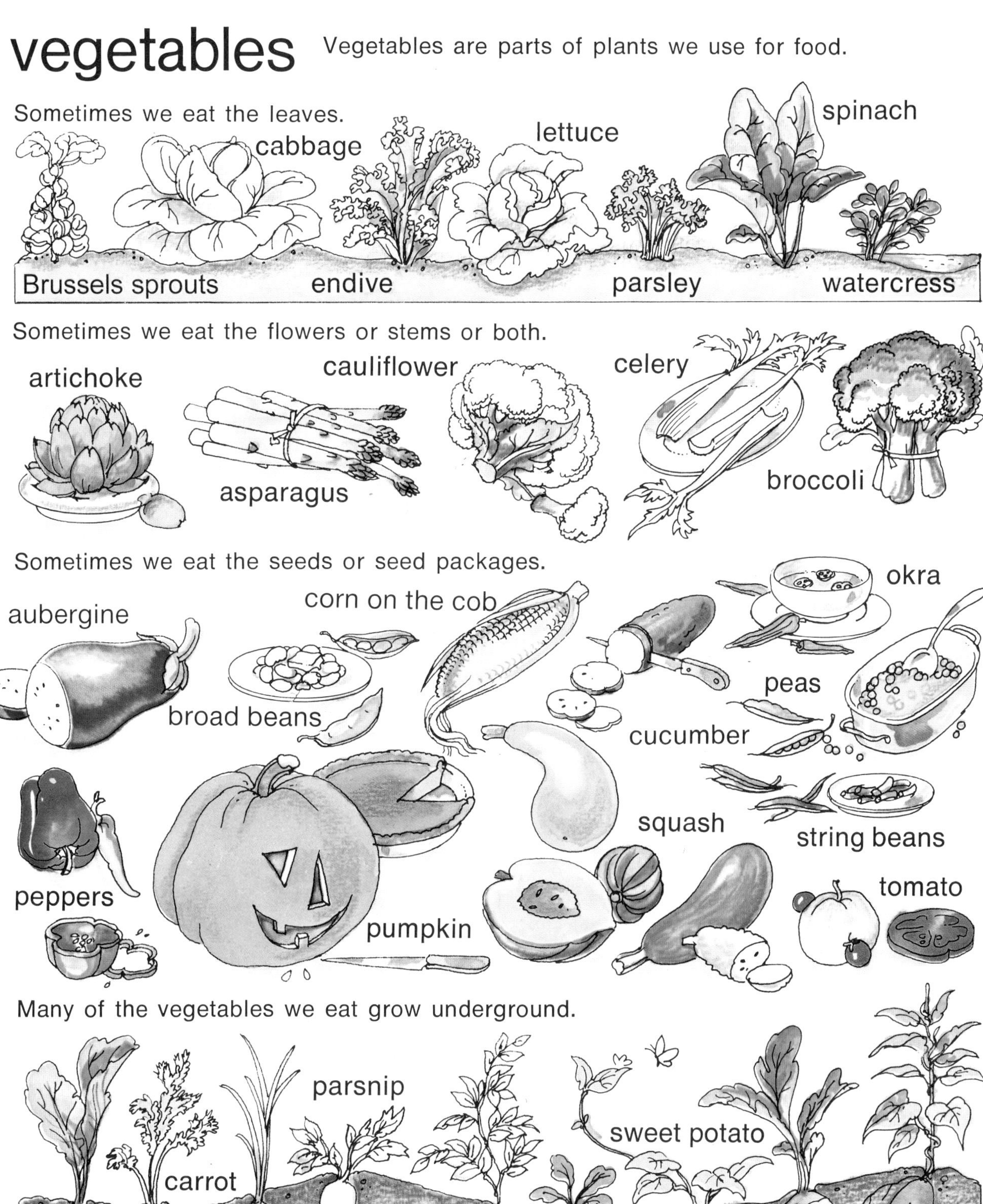

Sometimes we eat the flowers or stems or both.

Sometimes we eat the seeds or seed packages.

Many of the vegetables we eat grow underground.

What vegetables do you like to eat?

Wendy wears a witch's wig.

ABCDEFGHIJKLMNOPQRSTUV  XYZ

W is the first letter of these words.

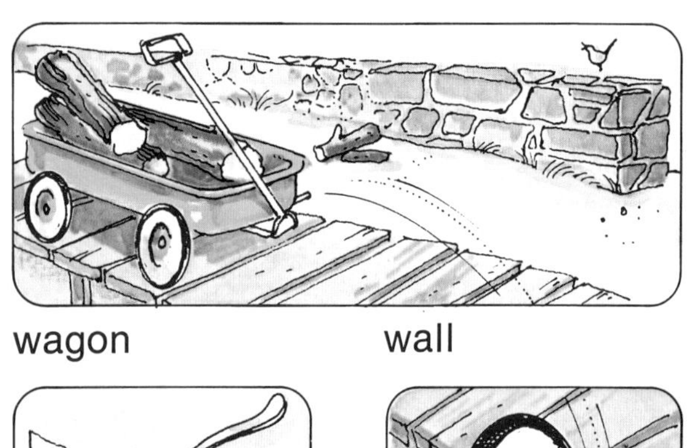

wagon wall

wallet

watch

watermelon

wheel

windmill

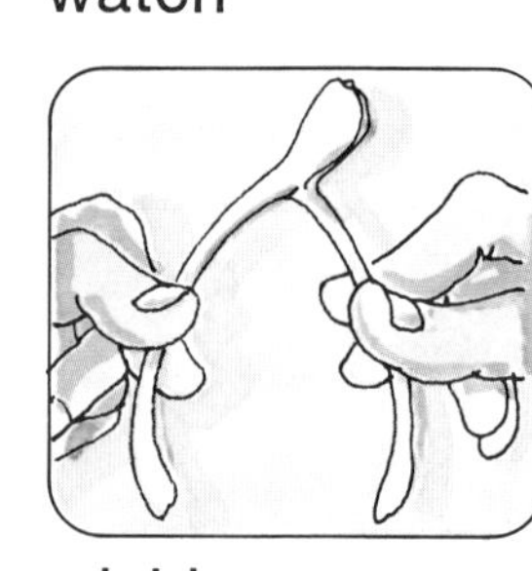

wishbone

wishing well

woodpecker worm

wreath

Which W words would you like to whisper?

abcdefghijklmnopqrstuv 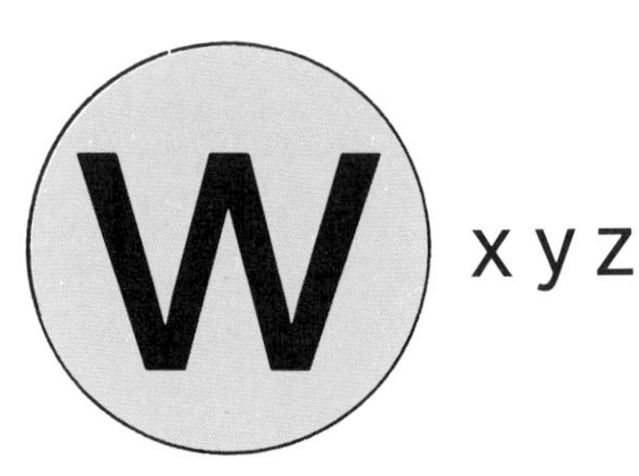 xyz

weather

The weatherman predicts the weather.

barometer
thermometer
weather map
weather balloon
weather vane

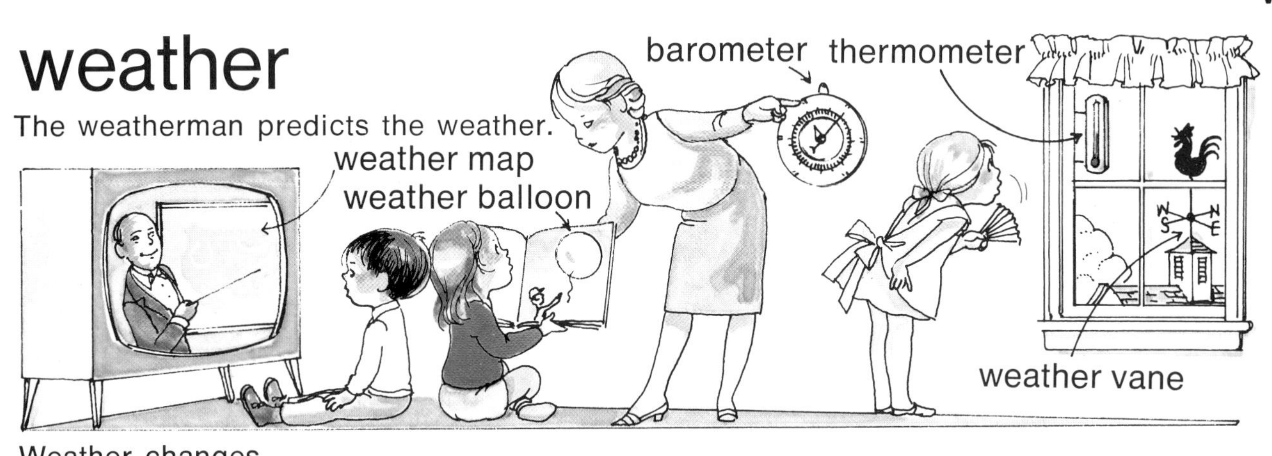

Weather changes.

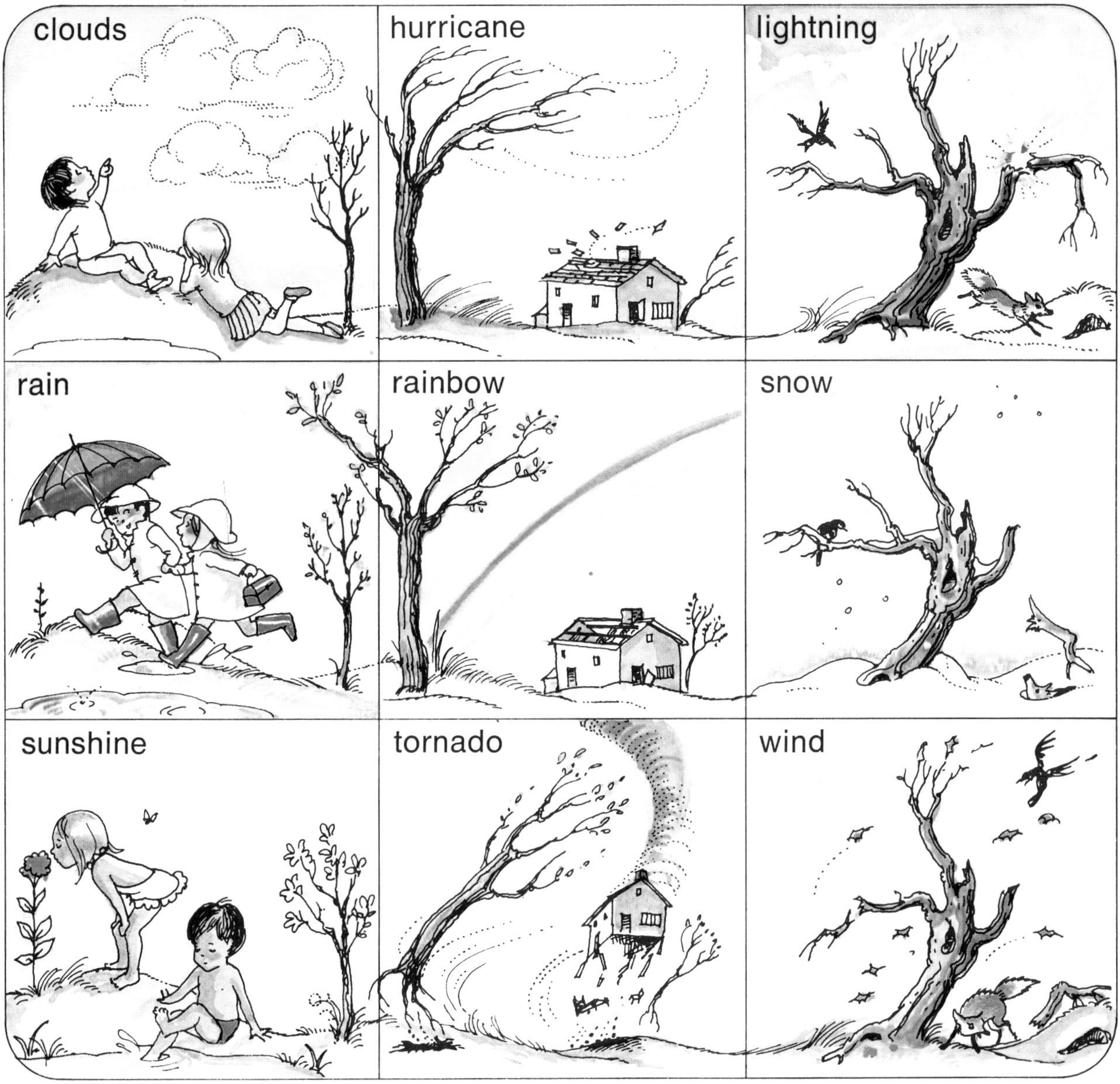

clouds
hurricane
lightning
rain
rainbow
snow
sunshine
tornado
wind

What kind of weather do you have today?

Writing

Here are some of the things you can use to write with.

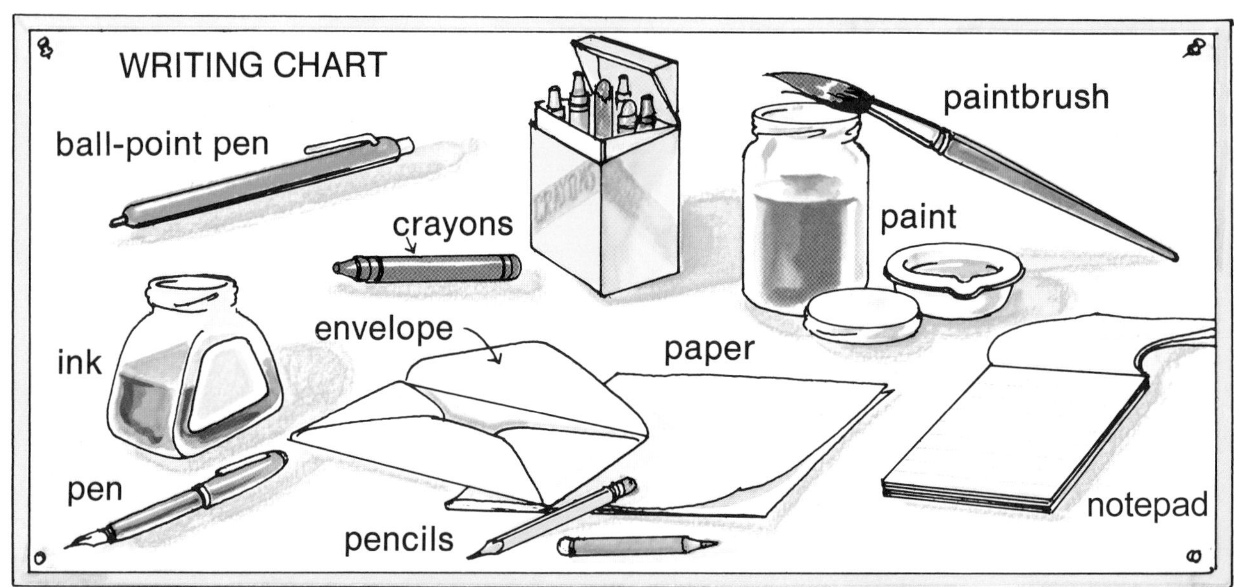

easel

typewriter

desk

chair

What do you write?

Xerxes examines his x-ray.

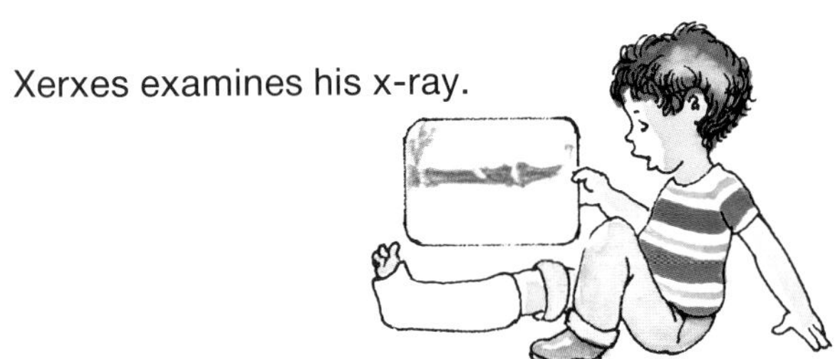

ABCDEFGHIJKLMNOPQRSTUVW X YZ

Not many words begin with X, but X is a special letter.
Can you tell why?

'Xmas' is short for 'Christmas'.

X marks the spot.

Sometimes 'X' means 'wrong'.

'XXXX' means lots of kisses.

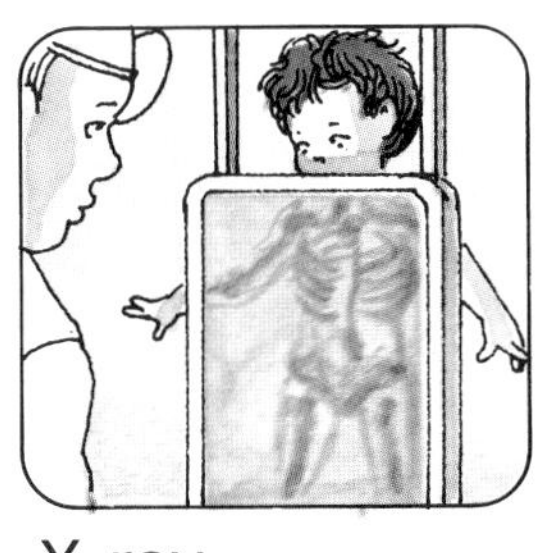

X-ray

xylophone

Can you think of some words that end with X?

abcdefghijklmnopqrstuvw

yz

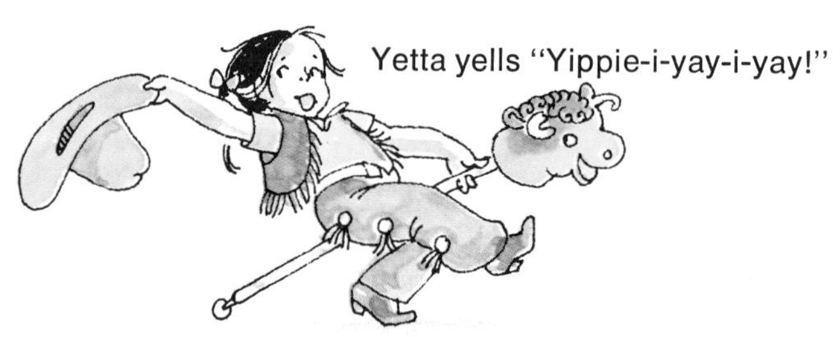

Yetta yells "Yippie-i-yay-i-yay!"

ABCDEFGHIJKLMNOPQRSTUVWX **Y** Z

Here are some words that start with Y.

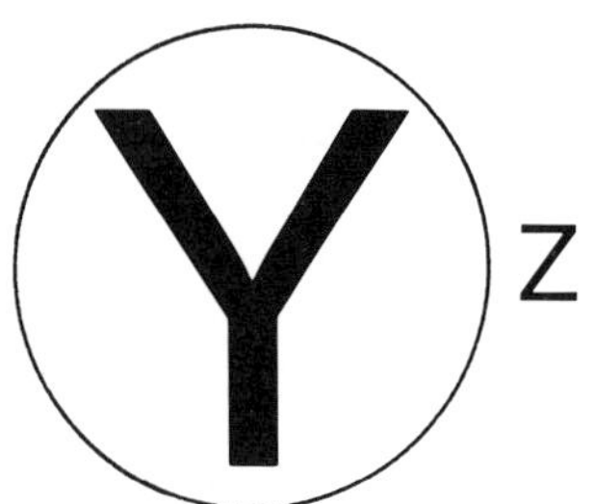

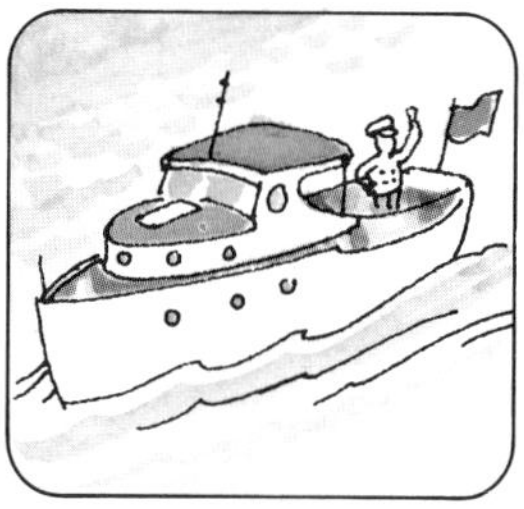

yacht

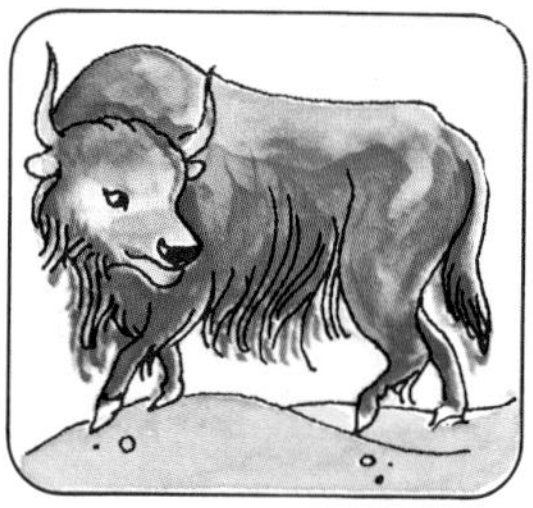

yak

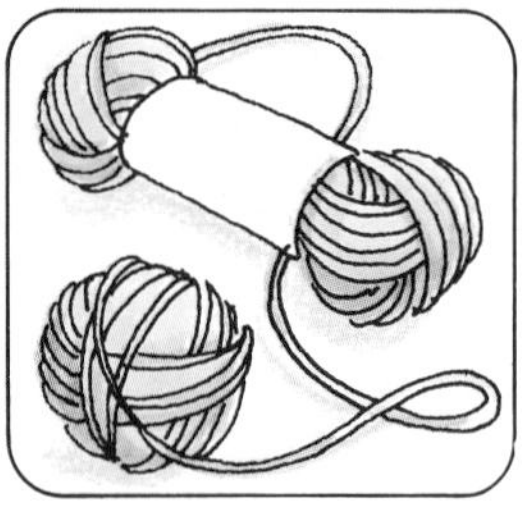

yarn

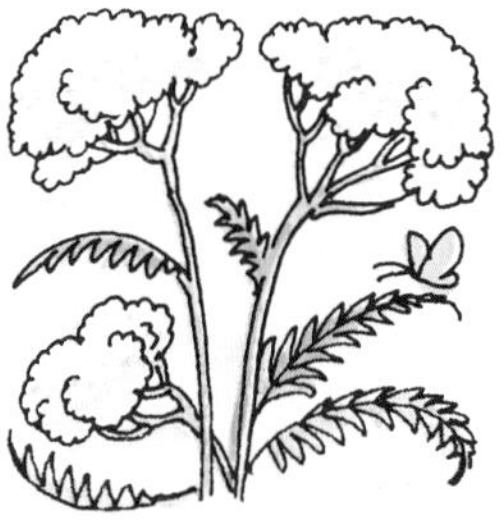

yarrow

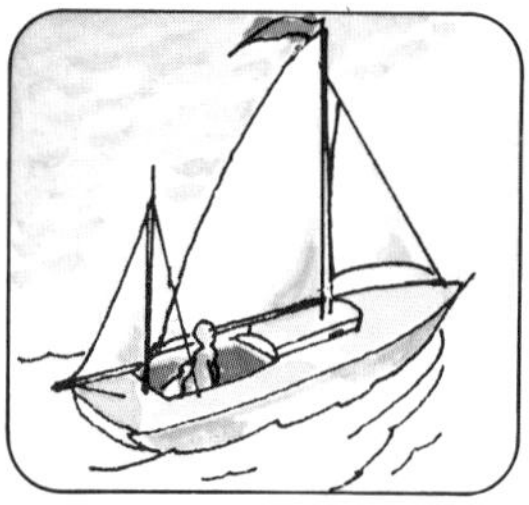

yawl

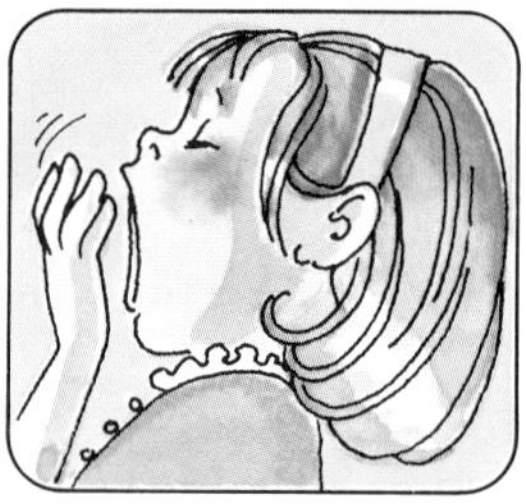

yawn

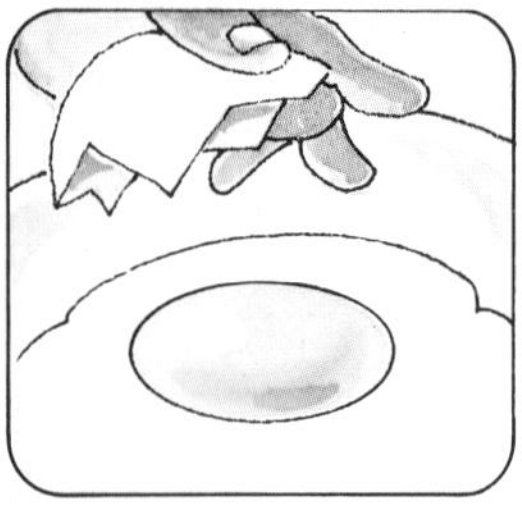

yellow yolk

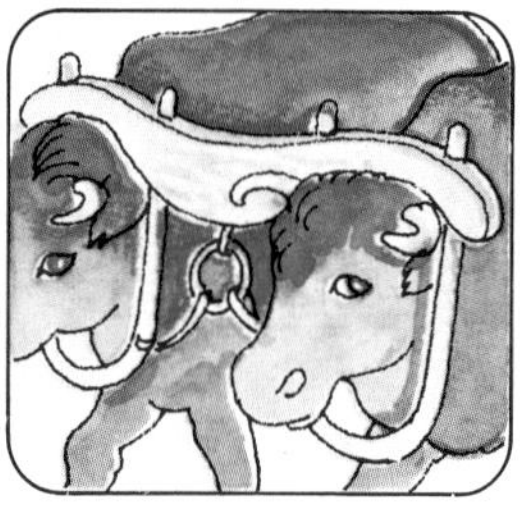

yoke

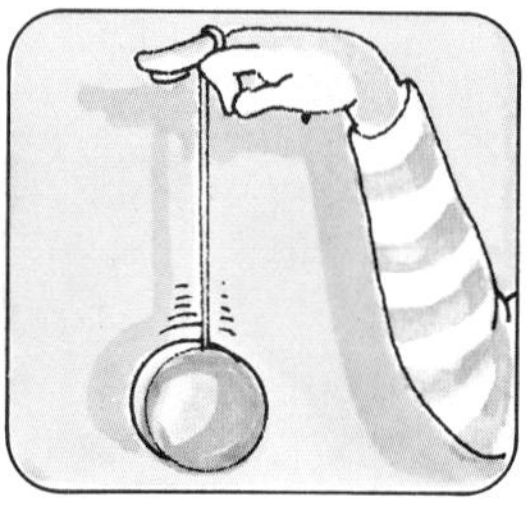

yo-yo

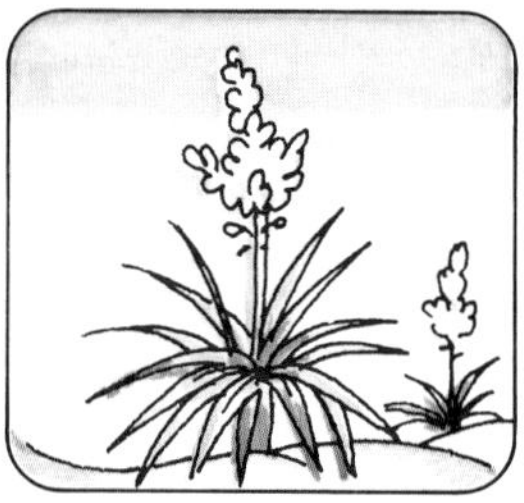

yucca

Can you think of any more y words?

abcdefghijklmnopqrstuvwx **y** z

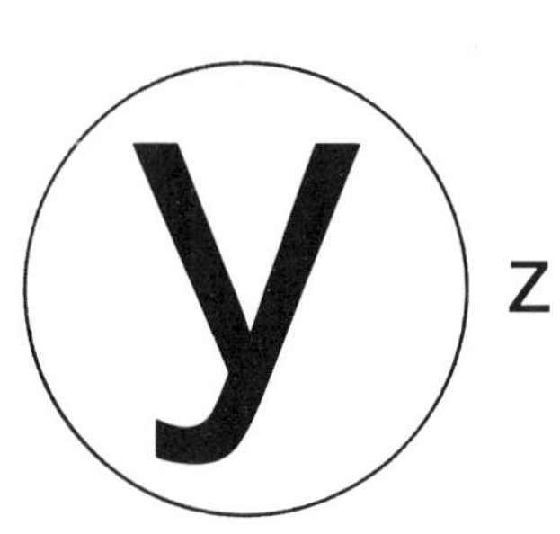

Zoe zips her zip.

ABCDEFGHIJKLMNOPQRSTUVWXY

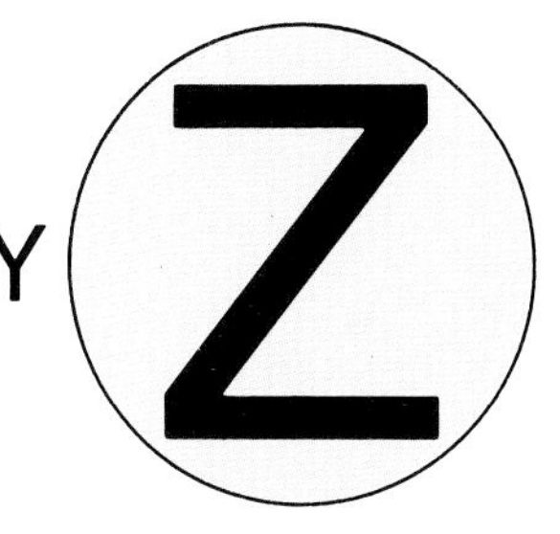

Z is the last letter in the alphabet.

Here are some words that begin with Z.

zebra

Zeppelin

zero

zigzag

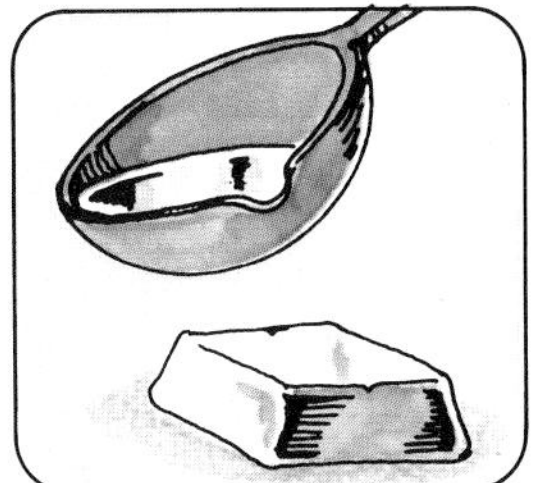

zinc

zinnia

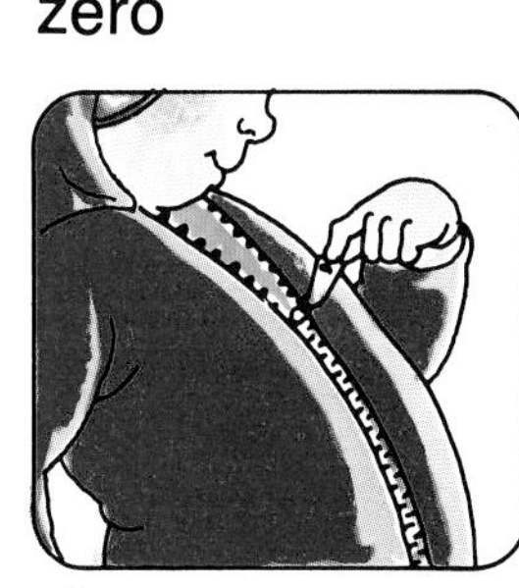

zip

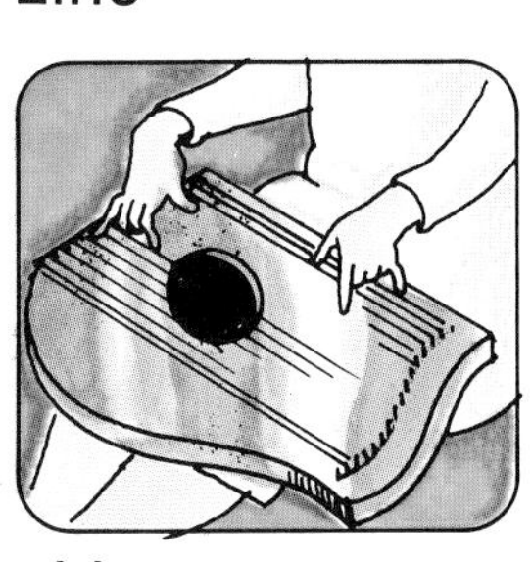

zither

zoom

Which Z word might you hear at the zoo?

abcdefghijklmnopqrstuvwxy

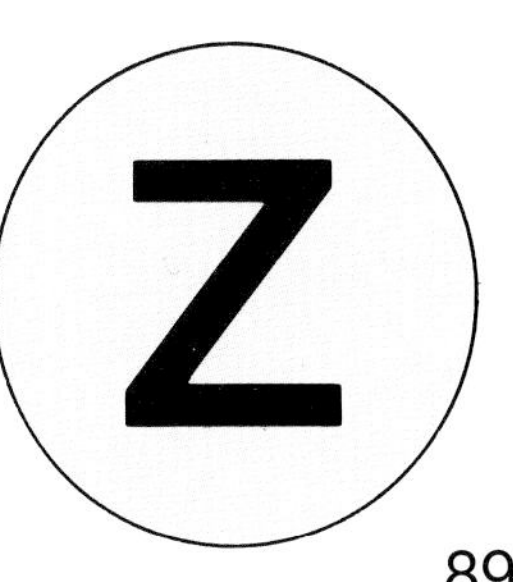

Z z

ZOO

Have you ever been to a zoo? A zoo is like a hotel for animals. The animals come from many parts of the world.

These animals came from Africa.

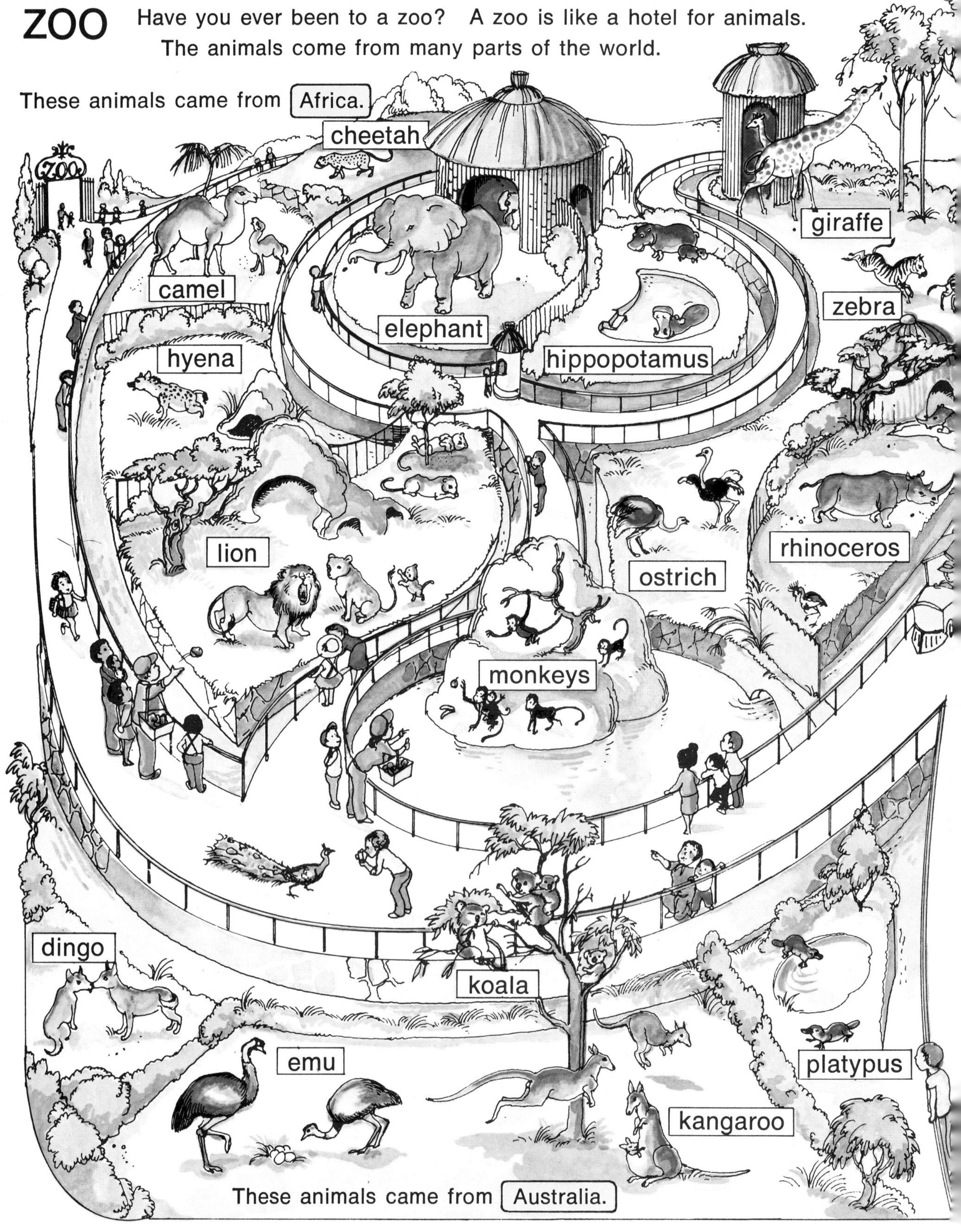

These animals came from Australia.

These animals came from Eurasia.
chamois
ibex
gazelle
cobra
tiger
polar bear
mongoose
panda
These animals come from North America.
caribou
bison
musk ox
grizzly bear
bobcat
anteater
llama
armadillo
ocelot
penguin
Which of these animals from South America do you like best?

Index

A
abacus 5
accordion 5
acorn 5
adobe house 35
aeroplane 7, 47, 77, 79
Africa 90
African desert 19
aims 91
air line 53
airport 5, 6-7
airship 79
alarm clock 75
algae 60
alligator 5
allosaurus 21
alphabet 5
American desert 19
American football 72
anatosaurus 20
anchor 5
angelfish 5
animals 8-9, 34, 58
ankle 12
ankylosaurus 20
ant 9, 37
anteater 39, 91
anthill 34
antique 47
ape 5
apple 5, 17, 29
apricot 29
apron 5
aqualung 53
aquarium 34
archery 72
arm 12
armadillo 91
armour 46
arrow 5, 73
arrowhead 46
art 46
artichoke 83
asleep 55
asparagus 83
aster 28
aubergine 83
audience 25
Australia 90
autograph 5
automobile 5
autumn 70
avocado 29
awake 55
axe 76

B
baby 42
back 12
baggage trolley 6
balcony 35
ball 10, 72, 77
ballerina 42
balloon 10, 77
ball-point pen 86
bamboo 60
banana 29
banjo 48
bank 10
barbecue 64
barbed-wire fence 64
barge 79
bark 61
barn 26, 34
barnyard 27
barometer 85
barrel 10
barrel cactus 19
baseball 72
basket 34, 59
basketball 72
bat 8
bathhouse 68
beach bag 68
beach ball 68
beach buggy 68
beads 77
beak 12
beans 83
bear 17, 77, 91
beaver 66
beaver lodge 34
bed 75
bee 26
beehive 26, 34
beet 83
beetle 37
bell 10, 48
belt 16
bench 57
bend 13
berries 61
bicycle 78
big wheel 25
bighorn sheep 45
binoculars 10
bird 11, 12
bird box 34
bird of paradise 9
birds' nest 34
birdseed 59
bison 91
bits of paper 23
black 17
blackberries 29
block of flats 35
blocks 71, 77
blouse 16
blows 10
blue 17
blue ribbon 25
bluebell 60
blueberries 17, 29
bobcat 91
body 12
bolt 76
bone 59
book 10, 14
boomerang 10
boot 16, 45, 64
bottom 12, 54
bounce 13
bow and arrow 73
bowl 23, 59
bowling 72
bowling ball 72
boy 10, 32
bracket fungus 61
branch 60
branding cattle 64
branding iron 64
brass 10
bread 27
bride 42
bridge 66, 79
broad beans 83
broccoli 83
brown 17
Brussels sprouts 83
bubbles 10
bucket 68
budgerigar 58
bugle 10
bulldozer 44
bunkhouse 64
bus 78
butter 10, 26
buttercup 28
butterfly 37, 47
button 10

C
cabbage 83
cactus 19, 60
cage 15, 59
calendar 75
calf 64
camel 8, 19, 90
camera 15
camper 78
campsite 45
canary 15, 58
canoe 78
cantaloupe 29
cap 16
cape 42
car 47, 78
car transporter 44
caravan 19, 35, 78
cards 15
cargo ship 53
caribou 91
carriage 79
carrier 15
carrot 59, 83
cartwheel 13
cat 12, 15, 58
cattail 60
cattle 64
cauliflower 83
cave 34, 35, 81
celery 15, 83
cello 48
centipede 37
cereal 27
chain 15
chair 68, 86
chamois 91
chaps 64
charcoal 17
chard 61
cheetah 90
cherries 29
chest 12
chick 17
chicken 26
children 15
chin-up 13
chisel 76
chrysanthemum 28
chuck wagon 64
cicada 37
circle 71
clam 9, 69
claws 12
climb 13
climbing frame 57
clock 47, 79
cloth 27
clothes 16
clothes hanger 16
cloud 69, 85
clover 61
club moss 61
coal car 81
coal mine 81
coat 16
cobra 91
coconut palm 61
coin 23
collar 59
colours 17
comb 23
combine harvester 44
come 55
compass 15, 76
competitors 25
compsognathus 21
conductor 48
cone (pine) 61
cone (shape) 71
control tower 7
cookies 15
coral 9, 53
cork 23
corn 27
corn on the cob 83
corral 64
costumes 46
cotton 27
covered wagon 46
cow 26, 64
cowboy 64
cowgirl 64
crab 69
cradle 15
cranberries 29
crane 44
crawl 13
crayon 86
cricket (game) 72
cricket (insect) 37
cricket ball 72
cricket bat 73
crocodile 9, 39
crocus 61
crops 27
croquet 31, 72
croquet ball 72
croquet mallet 73
crow 11
crown 42
crystals 47
cub 15
cube 71
cuckoo clock 75
cucumber 83
cultivator 32
cup fungus 61
cupcake 15
currants 29
cylinder 71
cymbals 48

D
dachshund 18
daddy-long-legs 37
daffodil 17
daisy 28
Dalmation 18
dandelion 18, 61
darts 18
date palm 19
dates 29
deep-sea diver 53
deerhound 18
desert 19
desk 86
detective 42
dictionary 18
dig 13
digger 44
dingo 90
dinosaur 20-21, 47
diplodocus 20
dishes 18
diver 53
Dobermann pinscher 18
dog 8, 18, 58, 64
doll 18, 77
dolphin 9
dominoes 31
donkey 26
doormat 18
double base 48
down 54
dragon 18
dragonfly 37
draughts 31
dress 16, 18
drill 76
drum 48
duck 18, 26, 42
dumb-bell 18
dump truck 44
dungarees 16

E
eagle 11, 22, 45
earthworm 9
easel 86
eat 22, 75
edelweiss 28
eel 22
egg 11, 21, 22, 26
eight 22, 51
eighteen 51
elbow 12

elderberries 29
electric clock 75
elephant 8, 22, 42, 90
eleven 22, 51
elf 22
elf owl 19
emu 90
endive 83
engine 79
entrance 55, 81
envelope 86
ermine 22
escalator 6
Eskimos 22
estate car 78
Eurasia 91
examines 87
excavator 22
exercise 22
exhibits 47
exit 55, 81
experiments 23

F
face 12
factory 66
fair 25
fairy 24
fall 13
family 34
fan 24
farm 26-27
farmer 27
farmhouse 25
fat 55
feather 12, 23, 24
fence 24
fern 39
ferry 66
fertilizer 32
field 27
fifteen 51
file 76
fin 12
finds 24
finger 12
fingerprint 24
fire fighter 24
fireflies 24
fish 12, 24, 47, 58, 69
fishing 72
fishing rod 73
five 24, 51
flag 24
flamingo 9
flats 35
flight attendant 7
flour mill 66
flower petal 23
flowers 28, 32, 61
flute 48
fly 13, 37
flying 24
flying squirrel 8
foot 12
foothill 45
footprint 21, 24
forsythia 60
fort 24
fossil 47
fossil eggs 21
fossil footprints 21
fountain 57
four 24, 51
fourteen 51
fox 9
foxglove 28
friends 58
frog 9, 17, 24
fruits 27, 29, 61
fuel lorry 7
fungus/fungi 61
funnel 24
fur 12
furniture 46

G
games 31, 72-73
garden 26, 32
garden gloves 32
gate 30
gazelle 91
geese 26
geranium 28
gerbil 58
get up 75
geyser 30
giant 30
giant fern 39
Gila monster 19
giraffe 8, 30, 90
girl 30, 32
gives 30
glacier 45
glass house 35
glasses 30
glove puppet 77
go 55
goat 26, 30
golf 72
golf ball 72
golf club 73
goodbye 55
goods train 78
goose 30
gooseberries 29
gourd 30
grain 30
grandfather clock 75
grapefruit 29
grapes 17, 29, 30
grass 61
grass blade 23
grass hut 35
grasshopper 37
green 17, 30, 61
grizzly bear 91
ground 32
guitar 48
gyroscope 30

H
hacksaw 76
hair 12
hair bow 17
hamburger 33
hammer 76
hamster 58
hand 12
hang 13
hangar 7
hanger 16
happy 55
harbour town 66
harmonica 48
harp 48
hat 16, 64
hawk 33
hay 27
head 12
headset 33
heart 71
heel 12
helicopter 6, 78
heliport 6
hello 55
helmet 33
hen house 25
heron 66
hide-and-seek 31
high 54
hikers 45
hiking 73
hinge 33
hip 12
hippopotamus 90
history 46
hobbyhorse 77
hoe/hoeing 32
hole 33
hollow tree 34
holly 33
hollyhock 28
homes 34-35
honey 26
honeybee 37
honeydew melon 29
hook 33
hoop 57
hopscotch 57
horn 33
hornets' nest 34
horse 8, 26, 33, 65
horse box 78
horseshoe 33
hour hand 75
hourglass 75
house spider 37
houseboat 35
houses 35
hugs 33
hummingbird 11, 33
hundred 51
hurricane 85
hyacinth 33
hyena 90

I
ibex 36, 91
iceberg 36
ice-skating 73
icicles 36
igloo 35, 36
iguana 36
impala 36
in 55
incense 36
incubator 36
India 36
ink 86
insects 37
inside 54
instruments 48
iodine 36
iris 17, 28
island 36, 53

J
jack 23, 38
jacket 16
jack-in-the-box 77
jack-in-the-pulpit 28
jaguar 39
jail 38
janitor 38
jar 38
jeans 16
jeep 38
jellybeans 38
jellyfish 9, 53
jester 38
jet plane 7
jewellery 46
jockey 38
jonquil 38
joy 38
judge 25
jug 38
juice 27
jumping 65
jumping jack 38
jumps 38
jungle 39

K
kangaroo 8, 40, 90
kangaroo rat 19
katydid 37
kayak 40
kelp 60
kennel 40
kettle 40
key 40
kimono 40
kindergarten 55
king 40
kingcup 28
kingfisher 66
kisses 40
kite 40
kitten 40
kiwi 11
knee 12
knickers 16
knife 76
knight 40
knitting 40
knot 40
koala 90
kookaburra 40

L
ladle 41
ladybird 37
lake 45, 66
lamb 41
lamp 41, 81
lasso 64
lead 59
leaf 17, 41
leapfrog 31
leaves 60, 61
leg 12
lei 41
lemon 29
lemonade 41
let's pretend 42
letter 41
lettuce 83
left 54
level 76
lichen 60
licks 41
life jacket 68
life raft 53
lifeguard 68
lift 81
lighthouse 69
lightning 85
lilac 41
lily 28
lime 29
liner 79
lion 9, 90
lipstick 41
lizard 9
llama 91
lobster 9, 69
lock 41
locomotive 41, 47
log cabin 35
lollipop 41
London Bridge 31
lorry 77, 79
lotus 60
low 54
luggage 6
lunch 75
lynx 41

M
machines 44
magic wand 42
magician 42
magnet 23
mallet 73
mammal 8
mandolin 43
mango 29
map 46
marbles 77
mask 43, 73
matches 43
meadow 27, 45, 66
measles 43
meat 26
medicine 43
melon 29
merry-go-round 25
microscope 60
milk 26
mince 59
miner 81
minute hand 75
mirror 59
mittens 16, 23, 43
mobile 43
mole 8
money 43
mongoose 91
monkey 8, 39, 43, 90
moon 43
moose 8
morning 75
morning-glory 28
mosquito 37
moth 9, 37
motor car 78
motorbike 43, 78
mountain 19, 45
mountain climber 45
mouse 43, 58
mummy 46
mumps 43
museums 46-47

mushroom 61
music 43, 48
musical chairs 31
musicians 48
musk ox 91

N
nail 23, 49, 76
names 50
nap 49
napkin 49
nasturtium 28
natural history 47
navel 12
neck 12
neckerchief 64
necklace 49
nectar 61
nectarine 29
needle 23, 49
needs 49
nest 11, 34, 49
net 49
new 55
newspaper 49
night 75
nightie 16
nine 51
nineteen 51
nomad 19
noodles 49
North America 91
notebook 49
notepad 86
numbers 51
nut 49, 61
nut and bolt 76
nutcracker 49

O
oasis 19
oboe 52
observation deck 7
ocean 53, 69
ocean liner 79
ocelot 91
ocotillo 19
octopus 9, 52
off 54
oilcan 52
okra 83
old 46, 55
olive 52
on 54
one 51, 52
one hundred 51
onion 52, 83
opposites 54-55
orange 17, 29, 52
orchard 26
orchestra 48
orchid 28, 39
organ 52
ostrich 11, 52, 90
otter 52
out 55
outside 54
over 54
overalls 52
owl 19, 52
owns 52
ox 52
oyster 52, 69

P
paint 86
paintbrush 86
painting 46
palm 19
pan 56
panda 91
pansy 28
panther 8
papaya 29
paper 23, 86
paper clip 23
paper house 35
parachute 56
parent 11
park 57
park bench 57
parrot 11, 39
parsley 83
parsnip 83
party dress 16
passengers 7
paste 56
path 32, 57
paw 12
peach 29
peacock 56
peak 45
peanut 56
pear 29
peas 83
pebble 23
pegboard 77
pelican 56
pen 86
pencil 86
penguin 9, 11, 91
penknife 56
penthouse 35
pepper(s) 56, 83
periscope 53
persimmon 29
petal 23
petrified wood 19
pets 56, 58-59
petticoat 16
petunia 17
pheasant 11
piano 48
pickaxe 45
pick-up truck 78
pier 66
pig 8, 26, 56
pigeon 57
pigsty 27
pilot 7
pin 23
pin the tail on the donkey 31
pine cone 61
pine needle 61
pine tree 61
pineapple 60
ping-pong ball 23
pink 17, 56
pitcher 56
pizza 56
plane 76
planting 32
plants 47, 60-61
plastic duck 23
platypus 90
play 57
pliers 76
plough 44
plum 17, 29
pocket watch 75
polar bear 9, 91
pomegranate 29
pond skater 66
pony 58, 64
porcupine 8
porpoise 56
porter 7
potato 83
pottery 46
pouch 34
pram 77
praying mantis 37
princess 42
prism 71
propeller 53
puffball 61
pull 13, 54
pumpkin 17, 83
puppy 56
purple 17
push 13, 54
puzzle 77
pyjamas 16
pyramid 71

Q
quail 62
quarry 62
quarters 62
queen 62
Queen Anne's lace 28
questions 62
quetzal 62
quill 62
quilt 62
quince 29, 62
quiver 62
quoits 62

R
rabbit 26, 42
raccoon 63
racket 73
radish 63, 83
railway line 78
rain 85
rain hat 16
rainbow 85
raincoat 16
raisins 63
rake 32, 63
ranch 64-65
ranch house 65
rancher 65
raspberries 29
rattlesnake 9
record 63
recreation 72
rectangle 71
rectangular block 71
red 17, 63
relax 57
rhinoceros 90
ribbon 63
ride 13
riding 65
right 54
right side up 54
ring 63
ring a ring o'roses 31
river 45, 63, 66, 78
road scraper 44
roadrunner 19
robot 77
rock 47, 60
rocket 47
rodeo 65
roll 13
roller 44
roller-skating 73
rooster 63
roots 61, 81
rope 45, 63
rope tricks 65
roping 65
rose 28, 63
row, row, row your boat 31
rowing boat 63, 66
rucksack 45
rug 63
ruler 63, 76
runway 6, 7

S
sad 55
safe 67
safety pin 23
saguaro cactus 19
sailing boat 69, 79
sailor 42
salad 27
salamander 9
salmon 9
sand 60
sand castle 68
sand dollar 69
sand dune 19
sandpaper 76
sandpiper 69
satellite 67
saw 76
saxophone 48
scales 12
scarecrow 32
scarf 16
science and technology 47
scooter 57
scorpion 37
screw 76
screwdriver 76
scuba diver 53
sculpture 46
sea 66
sea fan 9
sea grass 69
sea gull 69
seal 9
seaplane 53, 79
seashell 67
seashore 68-69
seasons 70
seaweed 59
seeds 32, 60, 61
seesaw 57
seven 51, 67
seventeen 51
shapes 71
shears 76
shed 81
sheep 19, 26, 45
shell 34, 69
shelter 45
ship 53, 69
shirt 16
shoe 16, 17, 67
shooting contest 65
short 55
shorts 16
shoulder 12
shovel 32
shrimp 69
sidewinder 19
sieve 68
silly 67
silo 27
single-engine aeroplane 7
sings 67
six 51, 67
sixteen 51
skating 73
skeleton 21, 67
ski 45
ski pole 45, 73
skiing 73
skin 12
skipping 31
skipping rope 77
skirt 16
skunk 9, 67
sky 69
sledging 73
slide 13, 57
slippers 16
sloth 39
snail 9
snake 39, 42, 58
snapdragon 28
snow 45, 85
snowman 67
snowmobile 67
snowsuit 16
socks 16
soil 60
song 67
South America 91
spade 32, 68
spanner 76
spider 9, 37
spinach 83
spinning top 77
sponge 9, 53
spool 23
spoon 67
sphere 71
sports 72-73
sports car 78
spring 70
spurs 64
square 71, 76
squash 83
squid 53
squirrel 57
stagecoach 67
star 71
starfish 9, 69
statue 57
steam locomotive 47
steel pin 23
stegosaurus 20
stem 61
stick insect 37
sticker 23